PEOPLE OF THE BOOK

Thomas Ulrome

PEOPLE OF THE BOOK

Two Novellas

First published in Great Britain in 2017 by Thomas Ulrome
via Type & Tell

Copyright © 2017 Thomas Ulrome
The moral right of Thomas Ulrome to be identified as the author of this work has
been asserted in accordance with the Copyright, Designs and Patents Act, 1988.

All rights reserved. Neither the whole nor any part of this publication may be
reproduced or transmitted in any form or by any means, electronic or mechanical,
without permission in writing from the author.

A CIP catalogue record for this book is available from the British Library

ISBN 978-1-78745-046-2

Type & Tell hereby exclude all liability to the extent permitted by law for any
errors or omissions in this book and for any costs, expenses, damages and losses
(including but not limited to any direct, indirect or consequential losses, loss of
profit, loss of reputation and all interest, penalties and legal costs (calculated on
a full indemnity basis) and all other professional costs and expenses) suffered or
incurred by a third party relying on any information contained in this book.

Type & Tell

To Penny

HOUSES THAT ARE HOMES

A Novella

HOUSES THAT ARE HOMES

Begun 6.6.91
Ended 12.12.91

Easter, Part 1, deals with a Christian family and ends at the
Day of Atonement – a Jewish festival.
(Roughly from Passover to Yom Kippur, 1991)
(Good Friday: 29th March; Yom Kippur: 18th September)

Day of Atonement, Part 2 – from Chapter 16 to end –
concentrates on the death of Ruth, a Jewish girl, but ends with
the faith of a Church of England minister.
(Roughly from Yom Kippur to Christmas, 1991)

The God of one becomes the God of all.

Part 1

EASTER

Chapter 1

The girl was pushing the boy in a home-made cart made of planks of wood with a wheel at each corner and a plastic stack-chair in the middle. 'Is this women's lib or does he push you?' a middle-aged woman in knitted hat called as she passed; the boy seemed not to understand but the girl smiled.

The man, walking behind the middle-aged woman, heard her say to the boy on a corner, brandishing a plastic dagger and holding a tatty black dog on a bit of rope, 'O dear, am I safe?' as the boy grinned.

The woman had stopped to hold open a gate to a narrow pedestrian path for a boy on a bike and continued to hold it back to let through the man: about 5' 10", with round, open face and set-apart eyes. Apart from the blonde curly hair, natural though appearing false, he gave the impression of being an amiable Rottweiler. In fact the dog with him was a cross, more Rottweiler than mongrel in all but colouring.

The man's name was Patrick, though he answered only to the initial 'P'. The dog he called Patrick.

He let the dog off the lead in the hall. He could hear his sister and her friend from the library sending themselves up: 'Ladies who lunch…' '… Ladies who cheese sandwich…' '… Ladies who cottage-cheese!' They laughed at their latest diet fad. Fat old gits. Stupid bitches.

At least it was better than her pontificating. In a pulpit, she was, you'd have thought, going on about some sin or the virgin birth.

His sister herself had just come in and was taking off her coat, gold ear-rings swinging as she threw the fake-fur across a chair, rubbing her hands before the fire as her colleague turned up the gas. She was making a cup of tea: instant granules; asked if he'd like one. He stood, swilling his tea in noisy gulps. The women sat, either side of the fire, his sister in this light astonishingly like Elizabeth Taylor: dark hair and brows, blue eyes, the swish of perfume, those incessant gold ear-rings, pendulous, flashing, animated as she moved. She was nodding agreement that Easter coincided with Passover this year, raising her cup to her lips, leaving a neat curvaceous red lip-stain.

On and on and on you go. O yes, you know it all. You make me sick! He caught sight of his sister's fur across the chair-arm. Lynch you for wearing a fur coat, lynch you for smoking. What about people who've been ill, can't go out, daren't risk the cold unless they've got a fur? What about the bereaved? O yes, you go on, stand there, condemning everyone, fur-wearers, smokers, then get into your nasty smelly automobiles and drive off, polluting the air.

He couldn't drive. Didn't want to. He would drive into the back of everyone, drive over everyone, like a tank.

He had pulled back the curtain and net and saw in the neighbour's parking-space, in place of the usual white BMW, the identical black one. He laughed himself silly at the concept: O naughty BMW! What did you do! You must have committed the vilest sin, BMW, to turn from a white to a black BMW overnight!

'What on earth is he laughing at now?'

He slammed the door, leaving the women, putting on his trainers out at the back. He thought of sticking a sign on the back of his stolen Reebocks: 'My other car's a Bentley Continental.'

Patrick raised his big maw but he shut the dog in, sending it cowering to the far side of the kitchen with a threatening elbow-lift.

The cleaner's bike rested against the wall beside the black BMW. Nancy-with-the-laughing-face or Cheerful Chops were their names for the cleaner. Even the cat buggered off when she was there, and she fed it. He fancied the cat with its black panther face. 'The psychopath of cats!'

'Poor woman. She's got her problems. Three sons out in the Gulf.'

The morning last week when roar after roar splitting the spring skies had made him realize that these were the pilots returning home from the Gulf war, in their Tornadoes, the very note of victory that suffused each swift flight confirming that these were men whose last sight of this land had been when they'd had to wonder if they would ever see England again. 'It's me, Mum! I'm home!' intrinsic, plain as a victory roll, the full history of each man's background clear in his flight: bachelor; young married man returning to his young family; the staider tone of the perhaps older Wing Co. The skies had been a translucent blue, one moment brilliantly illumined with sunshine, the next clouded over by dense grey rain clouds, heavy and thick, bespeaking thunder: although it had neither thundered nor rained.

His sister made much of the number of people she met in the village who had sons or nephews in the armed services. 'I knew it was like that in the Home Counties; didn't realize a village up here was the same.'

She was forever traipsing around the village doing good, wading through it in the February snows, making sure the old got their bread and something hot to drink.

'A good woman...' '...An angel...' '...Your sister is one of the good ones...'

Unemployed, friendless, he himself spent his days walking round the village.

He was passing the house with the dart-board pinned to the outside of the garage door: the garage set back, with plenty of room for their game. They had put it up first in winter, when hoar-frost had coated the wire and they had kept within doors: the exclusion of families behind lighted windows. Now it was spring, the holiday Easter, the weather by day dry and warm: assailed on all sides by the yellow of daffodils and forsythia, the red of tulips, fragile-branched trees heavily laden with pink cherry blossom.

He turned onto the crunching grit of an unmade-up lane, seeing through the late dusk the garden with its small home-made cross, marking the burial place of an animal amongst the cold-frames, the congested vegetable plot. The place itself, a bungalow, needed a lick of paint. Its front door was a sort of mauvy-blue and, on the yard outside, beside a pile of sand which bore each time he passed the same unchanging indentation of a shovel and the cement-mixer which he had never seen working, stood a purple Chevvy.

The garage door, damaged by woodrot at the foot, sported the same mauvy-blue. The peeling paint seemed chosen to tone with the Chevvy.

He had once seen a blowzy blonde cast him a look of suspicion as he'd passed her car.

He had visions of kicking the purple Chevvy as he passed.

'Why do you kill people?'

Why did you kill people! Huh! Because they had homes and lights in windows and people around them and purple Chevvies and mauve garage doors.

He felt sad by the time he passed a house on the corner of the pedestrian pathway: its lights on, a child asleep in the bedroom, the child he had seen helping her father lift out the cases when the family had returned from an Easter vacation. The father had greeted him one Sunday morning as he'd passed with his arms full of papers. The child he had once seen walking her dog.

Once he had seen behind this lighted window, part frosted glass but barely concealing, the outline of a girl, little older than this one, heavily pregnant, her huge stomach seemingly about to topple out of the window.

He walked under the tree laden with apple blossom.

And here he had seen, last month, the black woman with the swathed infant in her arms, snow-white shawl against black flesh, the cold wind cutting against her blown hair, her bare arms, minding him forcefully of some Western movie, as though it were snow that lay on her arms, as though she walked not through an English village but hostile Indian country.

He had turned to the spot where the path ran out at the road, on a corner. Every night if he walked past here about 8 o'clock he would see Neat-Beard in his kitchen, preparing food. Once he had even caught sight of Neat-Beard's black and white TV and, a few steps on, seen into the deep room of the posh house, expensively divided by what looked like pale oak panelled doors.

Houses being done up, with lights blazing, and banging within, and front doors and garage doors open; and roads up and obstacles in the road. He grew irate at cars on the pavement. He tore his hands and face on a rose because he refused to walk in the road to pass a pavement-parked car, though the road was empty.

And then he opened his own back door to hear his sister pontificating, 'What is it with these rich left-wingers? They seem to think that, because they're left, you won't notice they're rich and they'll be spared when the revolution comes.'

Chapter 2

'Well she had her breast removed five years ago...' She lowered her voice as P passed but he caught the drift.

Three women the old side of middle-aged, on the corner, blocking the pavement as usual. His own mother had died, years ago, of breast cancer. Grandfather, in a trilby, at mother's funeral: 'I've lost the best daughter a man ever had.'

...Mummies are dead things, all done up in brown bandage!

...Growing up, adolescent, with just his father: 'What's the matter with you? Admiring these people? They're *shits!* Drug-taking, drink... divorce... can't stay true to their wives, can't bring up their kids.

'What is it they're doing for a living? Making a racket! Vaw, Vaw, Vaw!

'Do you want to be like them? Is that it? Fancy their money? Listen, do you have any idea what it must be like never to have *one moment* to yourself? Never an unguarded moment, in case there's some bloke there, like as if you're royalty, with a camera, *click, click!* Never to have beans on toast, 'cos you can't afford to go around *farting* for *one evening.* Celebrity! I tell you, these celebrities, they'd give all they own for just *one evening* of being *Mr Nobody* like *you.* If they've got any sense they would.'

His father would always snap the set off if he heard pop music played when he was in the house. 'Load of rubbish: classical music being elitist. That same tranny that plays crap, you turn that dial there and you get Radio 3. £90 for two people to hear all of Beethoven's quartets. Six concerts. How many rock concerts can two people get to for 90 quid?'

He blamed 'pop music' – anything that wasn't written before

1826 – for his son's failure to excel at school. 'Don't talk to me about continuous assessment. Teachers just marking up the kids they know. Continuous assessment was what we had at primary school. And, because the teachers are so thick, it was the bright kids like me the teachers hated - not that I didn't hate them right back. The thick kids, the Philip Stickies and the Bob Shawns, they were the ones the teachers liked, they were the teachers' pets - cos they were thick, like the teachers, but they went along with everything the teachers said. Little Mister Master Goody-Pants. Could no more teach than lick my arse. Continuous assessment – Pah!

'And I'll tell you another thing. At least with grammar schools 25% of the kids got an education – you're not telling me 25% of kids get educated today.'

P picked up from the wall and drank a half-full can of abandoned soft drink. As revolting as the taste of Diet Coke, which was Nutrasweet on wheels.

Houses with green lights. Houses with red lights. Houses that looked like a tart's paradise. Houses with their drapes pulled back, even their nets: the house on the corner of the farmer's lane, shielded behind a thick country hedge: through it you could still see, at one point, the upturned-V revealing the house through its french windows.

He had seen a man here one summer Sunday, at work at his desk, seeming happy.

People in macs, hurrying through the rain to be home: man in a mac, outside french windows, struggling to insert his key.

The house on the corner, with its 6-litre Jag. This house was so big that, once when he passed, he could have sworn that he was hearing the sound of a party coming from the *garage.*

...His mother sweeping him up, himself a toddler, kissing

him on the nose: 'My little bundle of original sin!'

His father once claimed to have worked with a serial killer. 'That bloke who always used to escort women home, back off the train. "There are some strange people about. You never know who you might meet." - Linking arms with 'em, telling 'em there's some strange people about, then going and lurking in the shrubbery on the bank of some railway cutting, and leaping out on some unsuspecting wench. Strange that, isn't it?'

P had grown furious when he had heard: not *strange* at all, you ignorant *prat!*

He had to go to the shops for his sister. Before him in the queue at the check-out: the fat woman who calls everyone 'My love,' makes a fuss of dogs, treats kiddies at the Co-op; the lank-haired woman serving her equally friendly when he met her on the fields with her black dog. They were laughing at some tale the woman at the other check-out was telling: "'What can *girls* do that boys can't?"

"'*Girls* can kiss frogs and see if they'll turn into princes." And she picks it up and kisses it!

"'That one didn't turn into a prince!"

"'Wasn't a prince anyway."

"'*That* frog's just a frog!'"

He made his way through the bikes to the sweet-shop, where he was served by Sarah Keys while Duck's Disease weighed out a quarter of Nuttall's for Nancy-with-the-Laughing-Face.

When his father had died P had moved in with his sister. She was older than he by over two decades. She had no time for him: 'That one! He never has amounted to anything and he never will amount to anything! Yes, you I'm talking about!' she flashed as she passed. 'It's nothing but booze and drugs and womanizing...'

'When have you ever seen me bring home a woman?'

'Yes! That's it! You don't go with decent women you can bring home! It's all this... skulking behind bushes, or else buying..!' She raised her hand in half-threat.

He said, 'I'll set that dog on you.'

'You and whose army? He's my dog!'

The man watched his sister bury her face in the Rottweiler's fur.

He had lived with her for a year now. His father had died at the start of the World Cup. *Nessun Dorma* my arse. She was always calling him about something. 'You're old enough by now! To know right from wrong! Good God, you're nineteen!'

P's sister had been married, though he'd died. There had been some child. It had died later. So long ago P could hardly remember. She had lived for a while alone in her married home; for most of P's childhood, she'd seemed to be with their parents.

She worked now in the local library. The Greek she was studying was for a holiday. She did herself well, P thought: never stinted. 'I work so I spend it.'

As dark as he was fair, her hair was equally curly; though, whereas his was so by nature, hers came out of a bottle.

It was the only thing he had on her.

He set out to walk where car-tracks marked the field, surely the tale of illicit lovers driving here to indulge their passion nightly.

The boys on their scrambler motor-bikes, tossing unlicensed bikes wildly across the fields, roaring out onto the path, upon him, rearing to with skid-turns, revving away.

Psycho-path. Psycho-*path-y.* He laughed at his humour. *A*

psychopath is a catatonic who keeps on walking. When asked what 'P' meant, he liked to tell people: 'Psycho.' Sometimes he called himself 'Alf,' after Hitchcock, 'Fred,' even, once, 'Alfresco.'

Serial killers: those clowns! Nothing but serial killers this year: pieces in the paper, mini-series on television, Hannibal the Cannibal.

There it still was. He had first seen it in February:

The heavily-rutted path in patches was levelled with clinker; traces only remained of the mud on this frosty dawn. As the black-haired long-coated retriever bounded onto the field to the right sown with winter corn, the man saw in the hedge of old trees to the left what he had at first taken to be the leg of a man. The way that piece of wood just curved, like a knee...

He had grown up with a black long-coated retriever, or at least that had seemed the pedigree behind the mongrel pup which his mother had laid at the foot of his pram by his feet. '...And, by the time we got to Granny's, there it always was, on the pillow: little black face snuggled up beside your white one.'

...His pig of a sister, having a go at him for taking the Rottweiler out without a lead. 'I know he's safe, but you can't expect some kiddie strapped in a push-chair to feel happy when some big thing that size comes bounding up, even if he does only want to play.'

She loved children: forever bending down, chucking them, buying them chocolate bars or packets of crisps. P himself hated children, if he didn't hate their mothers more. They go yelping and screaming like kids. Common bitches. One of them was looking at him. Fancy me, do you? I'll give you something to fancy. I'll give you what for.

Pair of young women, he saw them every day, one blonde and one dark, the blonde one in tight jeans, cutting her arse in two, pushing her youngster in her push-chair, sometimes accompanied by a bounding dog. The large dark dog seemed shingled, its close coat a mess of tawny black.

One of these pig-ignorant sods walking with her friend and their brats in push-chairs walking straight into him. Bugger you! Why should I walk into the road! This one in the black mac was the worst in the village. He brushed her arm and body as she, at the last moment, half-heartedly swerved.

Chapter 3

'I'm stopping now anyway, the wind's getting up.'

'Wind likely to blow the last few hairs out of your head, is it, love?'

'That's right.'

Bill had moved in in June. P couldn't stand it. She had become more like Elizabeth Taylor than ever, squealing when she stepped on a frog by the gate, laughing delightedly as she saw a squirrel run along the fence and alight in their garden.

The bungalow with the mauve garage door stood empty, the purple Chevvy gone. Even the pile of sand and the cement-mixer had been removed. The garden was overgrown with nettles. P broke into the bungalow easily, pulling aside a cardboard strip blocking an already broken pane.

The house opposite was also empty, a *Sold* sign partly obscured by honeysuckle which, despite the wet and the cold, flowered in the hedge.

Without lights or electricity, sanitation or running water, P was unable to live in his squat independently of his sister's. He walked round the village alone. He felt lonely. He had developed a sort of friendship with that dog - the creature was big enough to lark with.

He was at his sister's, fallen asleep drunk on the sofa, when the stench of woodsmoke woke him. He drank from the bottle at his feet. The stench hit his nose. The house might be burning down around him. He fumbled frantically in search of lighted cigarette, lighted upholstery, lighted clothing.

The kitchen door let out onto the garden side of the house. The crackle of woodsmoke filled the air even here. Out in the lane, the smoke was sufficiently dense to cause choking. Sobbing seemed to fill the half-distant air. Voices rose and fell in the hazed stenched smog like some Greek chorus undulating its cry of pain.

The heat-haze was red. He thought that the fire must be at the top of the lane. He walked through to the main road. No sign yet of flame. The heat grew more coarse. The street-lamps hung, dulled, in the thick smog.

A man strode by opposite. A woman was entering a house at this side of the street.

He called over the road, 'What's going on, mate?'

'Thatched pub just gone up.'

The woman said, 'It's gone up. There's nobody hurt. They were doing so well, too.'

'Aye. Just got into the good pub guide.'

He returned to his sister's but all night could not sleep, nostrils rent by the pungent turgid hot woodsmoke.

Within a week of the fire, P encountered his sister outside the Co-op, exclaiming to a friend, 'But he was fit! He used to cycle! He used to go on sponsored bike-rides for charity – M.S. – He used to say you should help those who were worse off than yourself – O!'

She turned and told her brother, 'Alec from our Russian class. A fortnight to live. Stomach cancer.'

'O. Russian,' P muttered with a shrug, walking on. She had gone to Russian classes hoping to read Pushkin, Tolstoy and Dostoyevsky in the original. Her Christmas present to herself last year had been the new translation of *The Brothers Karamazov*.

His sister was devastated. Two small children – he almost lost his wife when his son was born. Always taking exercise –

judo-classes with his kids.

She berated herself for not having found out earlier. They'd been worried when he'd fallen out of class. His firm paid for him. He worked for a small specialized engineering company. The firm hoped to take advantage of perestroika.

...Alec and the other man in the class doing a knees-up low-kick rendition of *Song of the Volga Boatmen* in the original Russian...

The Russian class had ended last term. She had said to the teacher then, 'O what a blow!' Alec had never returned after Christmas.

It was half-over already, and still there had been nothing but glum events in this dreadful year. 'First there was the Gulf war, with Elaine's boy caught up, then I meet Jane for the first time in fifteen years and she's got her troubles; the *Pig & Ferret* burns down; I take the dog for a walk and the woman with the two terriers tells me the woman with the Alaskan bloodhound and the alsatian with a blue ball in its mouth has a husband with inoperable brain cancer, and now this.

'O but those two little kids! They've got to grow up without a father! The thing is, these days, kids think you get punished for things. They don't just think you get sick and die: they see all these films and think you get shot, you die, because you've done bad things...'

She talked a great deal to Bill, to friends in the street. She recalled him a lot when she was alone: Alec's marvellous manners – 'Manners maketh man' was certainly true of him... it was second nature – he could no more not stand aside for a woman to go through a door than fly to the moon.

...Alec pulling up behind her on his racing-bike, showing her copies of *Pravda* he'd got hold of to take to the class that evening: bright smiling face, a handsome man, father of those two poor children – while there's my brother, useless, drinking, drugging himself into oblivion... The narrow line between good and evil... She thought of upbringing, of circumstance, of how *she* could never have dreamed of doing some of the things her brother... Is it narrow or is it huge?

...But he and I were brought up by the same parents...

P opened the door to hear his sister still talking about Alec. 'You see the thing is there's no religion any more. In the old days you'd have said, "He's been called to glory." These days you turn on the box and there's some couple talking about divorce: "I mean, life's not a rehearsal, you only get one chance..."'

He poked his head round the door to tell her, 'He had his high point and then he died. "That knees-up couldn't have happened without me."'

She said to him, wet-eyed, 'You are disgusting.'

P had already roared to the dog and left. O I'm beyond you! I've put myself *out of the reach of people!* I don't have to listen to your *inane twaddle!*

He settled to sleep in the mauve-doored bungalow, his sister's twaddle bringing to mind the words of that inane pop-song, *The Streets of London*. He wanted to explode: I don't know what sort of person is expected to feel better because others feel worse!

No one had seen him break in. It was a quiet, pedestrian-only lane, too narrow for traffic. House-moving here would be a palaver: you could not get a truck anywhere near. The house opposite was still empty, despite its *Sold* sign.

He adjusted the curtains. Nothing lined about these – just cheap bits of old imitation velvet, strung precariously over the bird-spattered window-pane.

No lights in the lane. Broken carriage-light outside the bungalow. Electricity off. He had once known a bloke who could re-connect electrics, when the Board cut you off, and you didn't have to pay...

His sister exclaimed to Bill, 'If I'm not sick of death and destruction! I take the dog for a walk, I find that the woman with an alsatian's husband has a brain-tumour; I go to the greengrocer's, I learn that Alec's dying of stomach cancer; I stop to have a word to see how Mr Bligh across the road's renovations are doing and hear that his mother's had a heart attack; even the woman who calls me in to see if she's doing the right thing by her yucca tells me the dog on the sofa's got a few weeks to live!'

The woman at the greengrocer's had since told her that Alec had been allowed home for that last weekend; the children had been told. The older child, walking their dog, had seen it hare after a cat across somebody's garden and come home in floods after having been bawled at.

'And there's him, my brother, says that he can't see the point of living and he wishes he could die!'

She took the dog for a walk. From within the lighted hall of the bungalow of the widow who lived alone proceeded a gasp of effort, like someone straining to evacuate their bowels.

She tried not to imagine the fit athletic man shrunk to half his weight. O those poor children! What they must be seeing! What they must be going through!

She pulled Patrick away from another dog that he wanted to sniff at. In the dusk they crossed the road to the farm track.

No other dogs around. She let Patrick have his run while she stayed close to the entrance of the somewhat secluded field path.

She turned out of the track of a car's blinding lights as it sped round the corner at the top of the road. At least I was spared that terrible fear of knowing that Stan was to die. That poor woman knows that her husband has only a few weeks to live...

She re-fastened the dog to his lead and set off back. She still also, now that he was in his squat, worried about P. An aching heart is still an aching heart, whether it be a great aching heart or a mean heart.

Chapter 4

One day he woke up to the sound of a car driving onto the hard standing outside his window.

He pulled on his pants, sneaking out the back way, swaggering into the lane when he saw it was only someone who seemed to have an interest in the house opposite.

He stopped, amazed by the massive size of the rhubarb leaves in the garden at the top of the lane: one day two foot across, the next, he swore, a yard. They were not only green: this one, the biggest, was largely the red-brown of rose leaves.

A small mild-mannered old man was talking to another in his sister's lane. 'She said, "I'll fetch you some pads," so she fetched her some pads. Big enough to fit a bloody elephant.'

The weeks drew into months. The rain fell every day. The weather stayed blustery and cold, throughout May, throughout June. The weeds grew waist-high then man-high in the garden, concealing the home-made cross marking a cat's grave. Panes broke in the once-cherished greenhouse. Weeds threatened to cover what remained of the structure.

The empty house opposite remained *Sold* but empty. The parking of cars on his hard-standing had ceased. The white shrub rose grew tall, overloaded, along the gate-post of the absent gate.

He saw a couple walking, her hand, behind her, held in his. He wanted to stop their happiness, for it would never be his.

He entered his sister's hall to hear her say, 'I find, as I get older, the fish-wife side of my nature surfaces.'

'Her ambition is to be a cantankerous old biddy!' her friend from the library greeted him.

'"What do you want to be when you grow up?" "A cantankerous old biddy."'

'They kicked off talking about Yellow Jersey – that woman who's always first in the Post Office, pension day,' Bill told him in the kitchen, pouring out a mug of tea. His sister's voice carried through from the lounge: 'O no. You have to have flair to be a demon. He has a nasty streak but I have a demonic streak. To be nasty is not at all the same thing as being demonic. I am a demon. I have flair.'

The weather now was warmer. P took his mug and sat out on the step, calling the dog out to him. He stroked it as it wagged its tail.

His sister's voice carried out here. 'All this divorce you see around you, going on. What these kids don't realize is that television and film aren't life. They do it this way because they need to keep the story going. It's not clever or exciting or sophisticated. It's bloody stupid. You've *made a mistake.*'

He stroked the dog between its ears then took to flicking its ears in time to the various names he called his sister. The dog's play grew more aggressive. He stood, egging it to jump up to his chants:

'Potty Dotty.'

The dog jumped on its back legs to reach his snapping fingers.

'Nance
The Lance
Can Prance
In a trance.'

He laughed, shaking blood off the hand that the dog had briefly scratched.

'Nance and her Nancy-boy,' he minced.

'Nuncy-Dunsy-Runcie-Puncie-Funsy-Squncy,' he lisped.
She said, 'You're like a little kid.'

He grinned at her gat-toothedly.

The new warmer weather brought fresh grief. The smell of a barbecue wafted across the garden one Sunday afternoon: a summer day; still breezy; play on the middle Sunday of Wimbledon. The smell of car-tyres mingling with the realization, that's not a barbecue, accompanied by the arrival of a second fire engine, visible at the far end of the lane.

Still in her slippers, she ran to where the second fire-engine had now pulled in behind the first, in the driveway between the greengrocer's and the row of small new terraced houses, where lived the elderly ex-teacher who had attended Russian evening class.

'O! The old lady - is she all right? Have you got her out?'

The fireman wound up his hose beside the wide-open door of the engine which now fully blocked the driveway. 'I don't know. I've only just got here. Try through that door, that back garden. Know her, do you?'

...Piling into Bertha's car, on this very spot, to be driven: to Russian day at the village college. Once it had been Alec's car, on this very spot, Alec driving. And now Alec had cancer and Bertha was... '...She was sitting there, her face as black as a coon. At first I thought she'd been burnt on the mouth: her right side lower lip seemed to have a bright red weal. I thought, God, she's been burnt: why is she sitting here talking, why hasn't the ambulance doctor with her rushed her to hospital? She looked so thin, and black, not like Bertha: her glasses the only untouched, real, right part of her.

'Then I realized Bertha wasn't burnt: it was *soot,* all over her face, her mouth, her arms. She was sitting in a garden-chair by her garden-table, shocked, old and thin, in her nightdress and silky summer dressing-gown, pulling the dressing-gown to at the neck, saying, "Oh, I haven't even got a clean nightie on." She kept going on about, "The house is under-insured! I was saying only last week, I must up the house insurance!"'

She had run home, past ladders and hose and the great wide door of the fire-engine, to get Bertha a glass of water, unwilling to enter that charred house, stenched with soot. Bill was cooking their meal. The smell and the heat of the fillet steak in its heat-haze as he turned it over in the pan made her rush back. She gave Bertha the water. Bertha only briefly drank. Neighbours and earlier-arriving friends stroked her hands as she talked. The plump-faced doctor from the ambulance seemed in no hurry to get her into hospital, though there was talk now of taking her. The stench of fire permeated from the house. Bertha got up to go back into the house, 'Has the doctor got my pills? Have I given all my pills to the doctor?' The doctor and fireman seemed concerned: 'Better for her if she doesn't go back in there...'

Someone went into the house for her. She was led to the ambulance, firemen and police assuring her that they would take care of her house. Her daughters were away: one at university; the married one celebrating her first wedding anniversary. The police took details from a neighbour. From the garden wall where they sat could be seen fluttering at the front window the torn black remnants of the drapes. A fireman brought to the garden beside them the charred large double-glazing pane, the standard lamp with its melted white flex, segments of carpet adhering; the severely burnt chair where Bertha had sat: one arm burnt off, the rest charred, blackened, so deeply burnt that it flaked to the touch: you would not have thought anyone could have been sitting there and survived.

'...I'll tell you this, until this happened I wasn't sure I'd given up smoking for good, but now I know, I'll never touch a cigarette again: the sight of that chair...'

She had poured water for the dog into a saucer, having to go into that terrible house to snatch a half-washed saucer from the sink, though the dog gulped the water furiously. Now she sat with the neighbours on the low wall, stroking the dog and talking, discussing the cause.

'Perhaps she fell asleep smoking...'

'O yes. She did. The doctor – fireman – told me. She fell asleep smoking. In that chair. The lighted cigarette must have dropped from her hand. O! As if she hadn't had enough already! She'd been ill all week. She'd been on tranquillizers.'

A man said, 'Them tranquillizers is what sent 'er to sleep in the first place.'

She left as the fireman threw more chunks of burnt carpet beside her, feeling in the way, having left her address with neighbours. When, the next day, she saw the neighbours on their front lawn, the man with a Flymo, cutting Bertha's front garden, the woman said, 'I don't understand it. She was so happy. When she retired. Used to go singing about that garden...'

'Yes, she was happy, but she also said to me, "O, you hear of these women who don't get up till noon. I don't want to become like those women! They say they've got nothing to get up for."'

When his wife had gone in the man said, 'Anxiety. Not a thing you can do. Nature has to take its course. That woman's still grieving for her husband. I know all about anxiety, me. Had it meself. And my mother had it. Left alone, five on us to bring up, in the war. Aye, everyone's round here now, wants to help, while it's all *in the papers,* while there's a *bit of glamour.'*

She parted from him astonished at the notion of needing drama, excitement. Life had held nothing but shocks, events and drama this year, all of them evil: the death of a friend of thirty years at Easter; the fire at the *Pig & Ferret;* the abrupt end of Russian classes; Alec predicted to be dead of cancer within two weeks. Her friend and ex-neighbour status epilepticus, out for three and a half hours, in intensive care; and now this fire at Bertha's. She could not get over the sense of doom, especially at the fire at Bertha's: a fire-engine standing where she and Bertha had climbed into Alec's car. And now Alec is ill, Bertha in hospital...

'...the only part of her that looked like Bertha was her glasses,' P heard his sister repeating, '...smell of car-tyres. I thought to myself, "That's no barbecue." It was foam from the chair – the seat of the chair...'

P remembered Bertha from when he had walked behind her once with his sister: the elderly woman with good legs.

Amongst all this despair and grief, seeing people you know age visibly before your eyes, all that cheered was the sight of their neighbour's new baby, 8lbs 4 ounces, in his sailor-cap.

'Even the odd nice things that happen this year can't seem to penetrate this pervasive gloom. It is so... all-pervasive.' Expecting the doom to fall: *when is it going to be me?*

'...The tiny old man who used to walk round the village, often smelt drunk, a bit simple, used to go up to anybody and talk. But he'd take your dog for a walk, or look after your garden – he kept a beautiful garden, lovely apple trees, he pruned them every year.'

'...Face-down in the stream. What a nasty way to go.'

'He must have been drunk. Probably didn't feel a thing.'

His empty house, one window smashed, with skips outside and pop-music from within. P had passed a load of workmen, their vans marked with the colours of a damp-proofing firm. One Sunday he had seen some self-fancying Adonis stripped naked to his bronzed waist in the belief that religion was resurgent in the village, planning to pull some nubile rural wench on her way to church. It had rained later.

By asking around she had found where Bertha was, with her married daughter. She cut roses from the garden, including a white spray: deliciously scented, but fiercely thorned. When she arrived to deliver them, Bertha it seemed had been burnt after all. The beflecked layer of soot over seemingly a deep Mediterranean tan: colourant in the foam of the chair she had sat in. She was now deeply pale, and that had been a burn to her lower mouth: the whole lip blistered, as was a part of the upper, and a line of burn-blisters all along the side of her nose. Despite this she had not been kept in overnight. Her daughters had made arrangements for a private nursing home. The one at university was a nice girl, grateful, praising the scent of the roses when warned of the thorns; the married one, less pretty, seemed a bossy sort, eager to get her mother ensconced in the home. Bertha herself was perspiring a lot, wanting tissues to wipe her face with. She turned her burnt face to her just before leaving: 'Nancy, I don't feel very well.'

Chapter 5

He'd forgotten that it was Thursday morning. Thursday morning was pension day. Every Thursday morning they'd queue up at the post office and straight away afterwards you'd see them queuing up in the Co-op, the women with their shandies or lager, the men with a bottle of whisky at the till.

A line of old biddies, the women staider, though there were more men than women in the queue: glassy-eyed, up to their tricks, pretending to start a second queue by pushing in despite knowing for years that the post office queue split at the counter; or else pushing in by getting talking: to the old boy near the front to whose nervous tic his stick's juddering bang reverberated.

No one ever pushed in front of Yellow Jersey. The unwashed hair thrust inside a turban, sharp eye glinting above keen and beaky nose, she had been there a quarter of an hour before the post office counter opened, feigning indifference to the passing traffic picking up its papers, pretending an interest in the birthday cards.

P stood behind judder-stick flicking his giro.

He had had to go to the nearest town to get this: waiting for hours amongst dead-eyed winos, sockless women in open-toed sandals despite the bitter June weather, their new-borns wailing, their summer-clad toddlers banging the seats. The boy in the corner he'd been at school with. He'd slunk into his chair to avoid seeing him. Young men in leather jackets, hairless, ear-ringed, ostentatiously sighing or periodically rising with such velocity that they set the plastic seats juddering, half-flinging themselves at the counter, large brown hands splaying against the rim behind whose shatter-proof glass sat, imperturbable, the young, unsympathetic, female clerks.

'Why don't you get a job?' his sister had asked him. 'There are some jobs, if you try.'

P had never done more since leaving school than turn up for an interview, turn up and work for the odd half-day, 'three and a half days once,' some labouring job.

'But you've no friends. Men find their friends at work! ...by mixing with other men! You don't even have boozing pals.'

'Doesn't he have to be older to get income supp... social security?'

'If I know him he's lied about his age.'

She was too fraught to take much notice of him. The post woman who had also done a term of Russian, whose son had been in the Gulf, stopping her bike to talk, 'Have you heard about Alec? I mean, he was just a nice guy... He is a nice guy...' Ted, Alec, Deidre, Bertha; a dog with a fortnight to live, and the cat. The *Pig & Ferret* burning down. The woman with the yucca, worrying about her son, the helicopter pilot; and the woman who walks her dogs, whose husband has cancer. Renewedly, in disbelief, at times she repeated this list like an incantation. Elaine, outside the sorting office, on the step, talking of Alec's address and that of Bertha's nursing-home. 'O, and have you heard, the woman who keeps that shop, haberdasher's - her husband's got cancer of the brain and there's not a thing they can do, just chemo-therapy.' Throwing down and grinding her cigarette. 'I tell you, this year, I'm fearful to walk out the house for fear of what terrible news I might hear.' Neighbour at the door, 'I'm afraid I've got some rather bad news. I've just had Anathema to the vet's... danger of renal failure... no milk, cheese or cream, and none of the prawns that I've been giving her... Need to be cruel to be kind. The cat's going to hate us.' She had handed over two tins of special prescription catfood and a leaflet about cat nutrition.

She was almost laughing now at her list of woes: '...the people moving in across the road turn out to have a little boy who's paraplegic...' A baby on a zimmer frame. At the worst times it was as though evil hung palpably around the village.

From Elaine she had got Alec's address. On a mild July day she went to visit Alec. In bright crayon, a large notice was pinned to the door:

Only happy, positive, cheerful people are welcome here. Doom and gloom merchants can stay away.

There was no knocker save the letter-box. The letter-box showed signs of having been sellotaped over. She knocked, listening for signs from within. A similar notice hung on the back door. The doorbell had been affixed with paint, though this had probably happened some time ago. She stood, knocking on the pane at the side of the kitchen. No one appeared. She could hear nothing.

Returning at half past four with the fruit she had bought at Elaine's suggestion – 'My brother lingered a long time, but it wasn't very nice, those last months. He used to get very thirsty, at the end. He said his mouth was always dry. The best thing he said was melon.' - she encountered a woman in the front garden of the house with the notice, watering the bedding-plants.

'Excuse me but are you Alec's wife? I used to know Alec from Russian class. I heard that he wasn't well.'

Listening to his wife in their garden, a watering-can in her hand, relating the dreadful, frightening, frightful saga of the NHS – 'You're not an emergency! You haven't got cancer!' – twice having to resort to private medicine, a feeling of strong spiritual joy and spiritual succour began to permeate even before she'd begun to relate how they now relied on acupuncture and spiritualist care.

'The spiritualist says he's too young to die...'

'He is too young to die.'

A bronzed neighbour in cut-off jeans poked her head round the hedge to ask about that morning's visit to the hospital.

'Don't ask!'

'O, not again!'

'Again! I'll tell you later!'

Yet another doctor had had no notes, no history of the case, no previous knowledge of Alec.

'"O well, I'll put him down for another visit in two or three months' time."

'"He was given two months to live two months ago!"

'"What do you want then, two months or three? I'll put him down for two."'

The neighbour seemed nice. The whole atmosphere was good, on this mildly warm, barely sunny afternoon - good for an invalid to get around. Alec had gone to visit his friends at work. Tomorrow he was going fishing. 'He gets tired, but a couple of hours at a time... We take every day at a time, take it day by day... They said two months and it's been two months now, he's still here...'

'Isn't he having chemo-therapy? Aren't they doing anything for him?'

'Nothing for him. Nothing at all. I yelled at them after his operation, "You're sending him home to die!"

'They did an endoscopy – this was when they thought he'd got an ulcer – and they couldn't get the tube past his stomach.

They opened him up and found that the stomach cancer had spread to his liver and pancreas.

'He can't eat very much and he can't eat very much at once – his stomach's so small.'

While her mother talked their daughter was clomping about the path in her mother's shoes, a miniature watering-can in her hand.

I do feel uplifted, Nance thought as she left. I left that house in a different frame of mind. More, cheerful, neighbours had turned up as she was leaving: 'Don't forget to put the rubbish-bags out!' 'O yes! Mustn't forget the rubbish bags!'

She grew angry as days passed, talking to Bill. 'What's matter with these GPs? Can't recognize *cancer!* When someone has *two months to live!* We're hardly a deprived inner-city area! Within ten miles of here they split the atom, they discovered DNA! ...Talk of an ulcer, a barium meal – and he had to go private for that! The barium meal didn't reveal cancer – they operated expecting to find an ulcer, instead they found that stomach cancer had already spread to the liver and pancreas: "And it's the sort of cancer that interfering with could make worse, but by then they'd already done the operation." "O you're not an emergency. You haven't got cancer!" The man was being sick every day, he'd lost two and a half stones in weight! And this in a man who was so fit to begin with – do you remember? – he did that thirty-mile cycle-ride for charity, he played judo with his kids. Hated smoking – wouldn't even let his parents smoke in the house. "You're not an emergency. You've not got cancer." Well of course he had. The minute he went to that doctor's, he had cancer. If you're being sick every day, you've either got an ulcer or it's cancer. The man had already lost two and a half stones in weight!'

Bill said, 'It was probably already too late by then.'

'You mean they could have stopped it if they'd caught it earlier? Stopped it, or at least given him a few years longer – another chance!'

Already they talked as though he was dead: Elaine: '...a brave fight...'

Chapter 6

It was a very private place. The whole lane was quiet and secretive. Here Leylandii grew dense and tall, thickened by Lawson.

'You don't need to know where I'm living,' he told his sister. 'I come here to take the dog for a walk, that's all.'

'Aye, and to pick up your giro, and have your meals when it suits you.'

He went up to his old bedroom to get socks, sitting on the bed of youthful fantasy: '*"What are you going to be when you grow up?" "A serial killer."*' He had laughed himself silly, slapping his thighs.

He leashed Patrick and took the dog to the field-path. Hawthorn, the odd briar, a variety of ivy. Cats scurried from a terrier's bark. Birds could be heard flapping in the trees.

The path to the fields was lined with nettle and bracken. Elder here grew as high as a house. To one side stood houses; behind the other, an orchard. The hedge was denser on the house side, the buildings obscured even in winter by dense ivy over the framework of elder; the far side less dense, through which showed the orchard, a mass of white blossom in April through to May.

He stood at the edge of the path by a break in the hedge beyond which lay the fallow-field, knee-high in coarse grass save where rubbed flat by footfall. Diagonally beyond this lay another orchard, to the side and beyond which lay ploughed fields: surprisingly for this region separated by hedges, even, once, a small coppice. After a break there had been a resurrection of the regular car-tracks and of his fancy: two illicit lovers, meeting, parking a car after dark in these lonely fields. He dwelt on their nightly assignation: driving the car off the road, onto the field where by dawn its tracks bespoke its nightly presence. Did one get away to meet the other perhaps on the pretext of walking the dog: some slavering bulldog, spaniel or labrador in the front while they cavorted? P watched his own dog career across the field.

She went on and on about him.

What do they all want to live for? P wondered.

Why *do they all want to* live?

The greengrocer said, when told of her visit, 'It's not just the medical side of things. That family's not getting the support it needs, if their GP's not helping her. It's not just him, it's the whole family.'

Elaine said, 'I'd like to think I'd be brave like that. Well you've got to be, haven't you, when there's kids? You've got to go on, for their sake.'

She said yes, she was not so sure. When it happens... hard to predict: things catch up with you. Can't predict grief.

'He can't even drink like a man, in a pub, with friends! Skulking off, with a six-pack, on his own...'

P said to his sister, 'I once had a girlfriend who was a runner.' He meant a jogger had once stopped to pat his dog, then she'd run on.

'You haven't got the sense you were born with.'

Two days after visiting Alec's wife she looked out of the window to see the old apple tree, heavy with fruit, visibly collapsing, the bough bearing both blossom and fruit skirting the ground.

'So far this year there's been one death, two fires, two

inoperable cancers – one brain one stomach – one dying dog, one ailing cat, and one dead tree. O yes, nearly forgot, and one *status epilepticus* lasting three and a half hours. You've got to laugh, haven't you? Life's a black comedy. Go mad if you didn't laugh.'

She raised her fist. 'Filthy dog! Don't about people like that! There's two little kids, going to be without a father..!'

He left at great speed with Patrick, trying to run his fury to the ground. He saw these people - even Alec and his family - as fortunate, at least some of the time, for being a family, while people like his sister saw only the retribution they had coming. 'Two kids without a father!' At least they've had something good to *pay for*!

Walking Patrick at dusk down the field-path not far from Alec's, she found herself thinking, Aye well, she's still got her husband. Hasn't the least idea what it's going to be like when she's without him – how people's attitudes to her'll change.

At the time the old tree was collapsing, another had been afflicted with blight. The day after they'd spent the evening cutting back leaves and berryless sprays, a letter informed them that, owing to family illness, their long-awaited friends could not come from abroad.

Alone that night she began crying. I can't turn to anyone, all my friends seem to be dead. I can't turn to Bill, I've got no libido. She blew her nose, recalling, waiting for a stamp in the post office, 'Haven't seen you for a long time.' 'Aye. Eleven weeks.' 'How are you now? Got the lot over you, didn't you?' 'Both lots.' 'Both!' 'Two panfuls. Scalding.' Taking a fresh tissue at this absurdity, she thought of P: 'You have to laugh.'

He had no time for women. They were always wanting you

to do things to them. Always after wasting time doing it their way. He preferred to save time doing it to himself, or at the most dictating terms with the tarts he paid.

There had been a woman in some sort of pantomime outfit on the box last night and he rose in thought of her: flimsy white cravat down to cream sequined shorts, each movement sending myriad small silver discs flashing...

...The man and his daughter possessed identical faces: handsome, androgynous, differentiated less by age than by male or female hairstyle. It was so striking people would laugh, 'Well, at least you know *he* brought the right one back from the hospital!'

...Something else on the box... that violent fella... brought up in kids' homes. Couldn't bear to be touched. He would lash out at you...

He found himself thinking about his sister. His sister was a widow. She had once had a child who had died quite young. She would stand, one hip jutting, sometimes. She had a hip designed for hoisting a baby on. The dark-haired, blue-eyed good looks of Elizabeth Taylor. One bloke had even come back from a business trip to America with a bottle of *Elizabeth Taylor's Passion* when it first came out and she still had the perfume which she used for best, the purple triangular glass container buried inside its mink-trimmed cloth kept in her best handbag.

July was passing and still she felt low. Out of the blue she found herself thinking about the man who had answered an ad she'd once put in a free paper, years ago, when she'd lived in London. She had specified someone with intellectual interests. This chap had replied that he was an 'interlectual' who wanted a daughter, 'by adoption or by the natural method.' Abruptly she found herself thinking, my God, was he talking about child abuse?

...Those letters she had got then. The one twice her age, 'You wanted an older man?' The sad one whose wife had died of cancer; a spiritualist had told him, 'Her hair is growing now.' He thought this a miracle; she had felt sorry: for his pain, for his naïveté; for so many: that pain she had suffered struck new to each person, there was no way another could prepare... pain alone was its own initiation.

'I can't even feel sorry for myself - I look around and everyone's in a far worse position than I am!' Funnily enough it was the day she had to go to the dentist, while she was actually in the dentist's chair, that her mood changed. The dentist made her laugh by saying, having chipped off her two existing crowns, 'Now all we need is a power-cut!' She responded, after he had drilled for two more, 'I'll have more crowns than the Queen of England!'

Chapter 7

At first he thought that it was just the baby-seat pushed back; closer he saw a man's white shirt-front, like a dickie, the suit lapels agape.

He threw the book aside. Anyone could write trash like that. His sister had got him the book from the library. 'I do love you, you know.' She was always trying to get him to read. 'It would broaden you out. You've got brains. You're too brainy to sit all day glued to that telly.'

... 'Because what do you end up with when someone's illiterate? You end up with someone like him, that's what. Repressed. Can't express himself. Nothing but danger. No man is safe, with no outlet.

... 'Those men in chemical suits, in the Gulf war, sitting on the ground, reading books. They couldn't watch TV. They couldn't clip Walkmans to their ears, in those suits. They couldn't even listen to the World Service. They sat there, in those suits, with books in their hands. The only way they could hope to cut out the world, to cope with fear: books. Don't tell me books don't still have a place in the world. We're *depriving* kids: at seven, still not reading...'

P heard her talk of the builder she'd had round once who thought he was dying. 'Pains in his chest so he thought he was dying. "It's stress." Up to here with problems, people not paying him, worrying how he was going to feed his kids; some kiddie's horse kicking him in the teeth – literally – O you can laugh but it damn near killed him. Knocked him unconscious. He lost all his front teeth. He wouldn't go to hospital. Till he got these chest- pains. I told him, "It's stress. It's normal when you've been through what you've been through – you would be abnormal if it didn't happen." He told me, "I didn't know." All the TV programmes he's watched! TV! Newspapers! Land of literacy! Comes to showing him something that he needs to know – that'll happen to everyone: grief; bereavement; having to cope when you think you're going mad: "I didn't know."

'You can help people as well as entertain. By showing real people you're showing things real people need to know. With all these car chases, all you're doing is encouraging kids to steal cars.

'There's no decency any more. Books – films, TV, should give people a *centre*. So much of the press is: *cut off! Dismiss!* He's mad! Lost his wits! He doesn't count! None of it tells you how to cope when you think you are losing your wits, when you are still alive – how to struggle on, get through, achieve some peace of mind. That's what books do - or did. This is real! That's how it is! Real life! Not: O, he's mad, dismiss that crazy man, cut him out of life!'

'You never talk about something important: the bomb... the environment ...' P complained to his sister, though both topics bored him rigid.

'I've never believed the bomb would be used. As for the environment, I don't drive a car. Now shut up and eat your lettuce,' she told him, thrusting before him a plate of chips and hamburger.

She said to him as she bustled in the kitchen, 'No, youngsters today, you don't take me in. I've never thought youth did have all the answers. You think you know a lot, but it's all parrot-fashion: don't smoke, they tell you at school, and half of you turn your nose up at any poor devil caught smoking; but O, drink, that's all right. As for cars, everybody has a car.'

She sat down opposite him with her own plateful. 'I feel

sorry for youngsters actually. They tell you it's the best time of your life. It's not. It's the worst. Gets better as you get older. Life does.' She picked up his guzzled plate.

A couple of friends her own age in the village had sons who were divorced, both after short marriages. One had her son back living with her; the other made him invest his money from the sale of a property into another house. 'It's not in nature. A bird doesn't return to the nest.' Both divorces had been sudden, a shock. In both cases the wife seemed to have found someone else or to have walked out.

'"I've got the right to live with the man I love," these whingers and whiners belly-ache on. Aye, and your child's got the right to grow up with his father!'

He had once heard her say to a friend from the library, 'I mean, won the Nobel Prize, he's supposed to understand *character*, yet he's been married and divorced five times!'

'Well everyone's entitled to make a mistake...'

'Not five times they're not! All his female characters – they're just men in skirts. "Her first two marriages were just husband material." No woman sees a man like that! *No* woman has *ever* seen a man as *husband material!*'

P had heard her tell her friend from the library, 'Nobody has to get married these days. There's no shotguns any more. And most people do stay married. One-third end in divorce. That means two-thirds don't. Two-thirds don't, when divorce is easy. You see, how it is, the old ways are still the norm. Some of these youngsters want telling that Hollywood writes screenplays this way because the story must go on: marriage, divorce. It isn't real life, it's just some bastard making a living.' Her friend laughed as she'd put her key in the door.

Her father had said of her, 'Comes from working in library,

y'see. Nowt to do but sit and read papers all day.'

She was not above saying to Bill, 'Ain't I daft! I'm the daftest little critter in Christendom!'

They would lie in bed on a Sunday, dissecting the *Sunday Times.*

'Got the fucks?'

'Yup. Here's the *tarts* with the *fucks* in the middle,' Bill said, passing her the arts section with the books inside.

They were forever carrying on like this. He'd seen them. They were capable of lying in bed inventing names for thrillers:

Murder Least Foul

And So to Dead

Bill had laughed at Reader, I Murdered Him, but this turned out to be the name of a real book.

P filled with fear at the way things were developing between Bill and his sister.

He came on them one day laughing over a wedding picture in the local paper, the man thin and seedy, she a size 20.

'He looks hung-over. Doesn't know his own collar-size! God knows what size her collar would be if she had one. Looks like they've both been married before - yes, look, they have: bride's daughters, groom's daughters: bridesmaids. But they've gone the whole hog: a white wedding. She's been *given away!* ...and look, O look, I don't believe this, this is pure Plum: the best man is the groom's *carpet-bowls partner!* But how romantic – they're keeping the honeymoon secret!'

P overheard this. He felt taut with fury. He thought fat-cow baldilocks was going to ask her to marry him.

Chapter 8

Turning the corner, P saw a car draw up outside a house. It was playing what seemed at first loud opera music. A blond young man got out. Another young man who had been knocking on the door of the house turned away to his own car in the drive and greeted the blond youth:

'Ny chance of going back to the Valley then?'

'Bad as that is it?'

'Yea.'

Walking past in the evening sunshine on the far side of the road, P wondered what the Valley was. A place? A disco? A hostel? Why could he not stay at home? The darker man failing to make up a quarrel with his parents; his friend, the blond man, arriving in the midst of this? Almost round the corner, P looked back at the sound of another knock on the house door. ...Perhaps not a friend but his brother. P felt a stab of bitter loss at having no brother of his own.

P had had a friend, Mark, but he had banged up some girl at a party and ever thereafter gone whining on about a father's right to see his kiddie.

'Children are always a disappointment,' P had told him. 'I don't understand why anybody has them.'

He felt this every time he saw kids on TV or spied over a shoulder somebody's magazine or saw in real life a family scene of adults fussing over a pram.

It always struck him as incredible that parents could love their children - or, for that matter, that children could love their parents.

Mark wore his dark hair scraped into a pony-tail, baggy blue jeans, and an even baggier off-black sweater.

'No wonder they don't want him in the family,' Bill had said. 'Who'd want him as a provider?'

'O he's all right. He's just a kid. At least he's got more about him than our P has.'

'I should think even P could bang a girl up at a party.'

Mark had once visited P at his sister's: sitting talking about his child's mother's family. Mark had not been allowed near to see the baby, though P had seen it once, with his sister. They had been out together one cold wintry evening. The child's grandfather had been behind them at the post office, thanking P's sister for her congratulations card.

'Would you like to come and see the baby?'

He had entered with her a glowing warm room lit by a log fire. Here sat the man's three daughters, the middle one of whom suckled an infant. Beneath the chair of the youngest, a small new puppy nestled asleep beside the fire's warmth.

On the settee sat an old biddy, the man's mother. This stern erect church-goer, Christian to the bone, could not, he had told them, have been more pleased by the new child in her house.

'That's what I mean,' Mark had told him after. '*They* drop all morals. *They* get everything. The child is *all theirs*. The father has no rights. I mean, why should that *old biddy* have more rights to my child than *I* do, its *father?*'

P soon grew bored with such talk.

Mark had asked him after that initial meeting, 'Did you see her? What was she like?'

P had no impression save of a baby, alike to all others save for the erectness of its neck.

Now here sat Mark, going on about his straight-necked

baby. 'I think it was her. In the street. P, I've *seen* her! Patty wasn't with her - She was with an old woman - could that be his mother? - but I'm sure the girl with her, pushing her, was Patty's little sister!

'O P, was it her?

'O, I think it was!

'O, she's glorious!

'I remembered what you'd said, about the neck, and that's it, she did have ever such a straight neck, not like other babies...'

P had stopped listening, remembering the conversation between the man and his sister in that winter house: 'We do know who the father is, but he's not a nice man; she's decided she doesn't want anything to do with him.'

'Aye, not a nice man he might be,' declared P's sister, recounting the incident angrily to Bill. 'He's nice enough for her to have slept with him; nice enough for her to go through with having his child! "A bad lot... been inside..." What right have they? To deprive that child of its father. And what about *him* – no chance to stand by her. I tell you, sometimes men are right to feel aggrieved.'

Chapter 9

She was in the bath, drying herself, when she heard the knock.

'There's someone at the door,' she called out to Bill.

'It's some fart selling something.' He came back and told her, 'No we are not having thin dish-cloths this year!'

She laughed mildly. Poor boys. On some Youth Training mission. They came every year, clutching their cards; one claiming to be an epileptic; one, big, cheerful, black, making it a joy to be flogged rubbish by him. Why couldn't they give them *decent* tea-towels to sell? The saddest had been, in the depth of winter, one boy, alone, shuddering, hurt, expecting to fail, lacking even a coat.

She was wearing some sort of knitted top of bobbly cotton, lace-patterned across the bust, with wavy edging at the neck. As she bent down, her pearls hanging, white brassiere showing through the lace, perfume breathed off her. P breathed it from the breasts above, urging him to put up his hand and grasp the firm round tit, like a melon, a grape-fruit, a rugger-ball – he'd shot up; it was almost bursting out of him.

'Where are you going now? I've just given you your tea!'

P had shot up, under her arm, out of the house, back to his squat.

He had started telling people she was his mother.

'I'm not your mother! I'm your sister! What put that daft idea into your head?'

Beneath the suffocating breasts, the sharp-sweet perfume overwhelming, pendulous gold ear-ring skirting his mouth.

The papers were full of serial killers, attacks on women, American mayhem, what to do if attacked on a tube-train.

...'There's no *humour* in it. I mean, you never hear of people going into analysis for a knees-up. I agree there's more to people than meets the eye - but there's not that much more is what I'm saying.'

...The bored young man on a Saturday night in trainers and jeans and anorak, Walkman to his ears, still really a schoolboy, with nowhere to go, pretending it didn't matter; older youths, jaunty of step, in jackets and ties.

... 'My God, young people nowadays! The whiskery old tramp in the distance with his pants in gathers round his ankles turns out to be some designer-clad youth with a pig-tail dressed in the height of fashion!'

Raised voices at the top of his sister's lane. Two women, one thirty-ish with toddlers, the other fiftyish with a bike, each waving a finger at the other.

'I've got two children and I was hurrying to catch the bank!'

'I've had three children!' Cycling away, she called out, 'Cow!'

'Hope you fall off!'

'And you!'

The smell of dust thrust up from hot pavements by heavy rain.

The queue at the post office counter. A small, plump old woman stood eyeing a tiny child. Eventually she said, 'Hello!'

'Say hello to the lady.' The mother's voice was slightly foreign.

'Hello.'

'That's a nice hat.'

'My hat.'

'Can I have your hat? It wouldn't fit me, would it?'

'Say no.'

'What's that?' asked the child.

'The lady is wearing a stick.'

'Would you like my stick? Say, no thank you, you don't want that! I have to have this. I've got a bone in my knee.'

'O poor lady,' said the mother.

'Does the lady cry?'

'No, I don't cry very much these days. They grow up so quickly, don't they? I've got two grandchildren her age, but my grandchildren are in Cornwall. I hardly ever see them.'

'You must miss them very much.'

'I do miss them. This time when they're young goes by so quickly.'

'And they'll miss you.'

'O I don't know.'

'O they will.'

'They say they miss me. I've another one in Fowl's Hill, just round the corner, twenty-one he is, but never comes to see me, he's got no time for his old gran.'

'He will have. Another year or so. When he's setting up. Then it'll be all, "Gran, how do I do this?" and "Gran how do I do that?"'

He liked strangling people. 'It's ever so easy. It just goes pop and then that's it.'

There had been another murder, young woman student, this one a beauty, wearing enormous gold dangly ear-rings.

... 'That's your hang-up, not mine.'

'God, don't be tedious! The last bloke who talked like that was that serial killer in the TV serial the other day.'

He had got up and left the house and walked alone in the middle of the night. *O no, I shan't go mad. Whatever else today has taught me, it is that I shall not go mad. But I might well kill someone.*

He had watched the two-part television version of the Ted

Bundy serial murders. He thought that he should go to Florida to commit a killing, that he too might be granted the grace of the electric chair.

Sound of cars and trains. Cold. He pulled his mac more tightly round him.

God of mercy. God of love. The thing is, if it did happen, you've made it so desired, so unattainable that, by now, if it did happen, it would be a miracle, not of this earth. Paradise.

'...the papers full of pictures of Anthony Hopkins with blood round his mouth! And *this* they call *art!*'

P had arrived at his sister's to hear Bill telling friends how they'd met.

'I met her on the top of a bus.'

'*You!* A *bus!*'

'The car was in for service. Some drunk was being obstreperous. He half-fell across her. She was shocked, so I invited her for a drink. And that's how we met.'

The friends had laughed when he'd called her a chatterbox.

'Well at least it's better than him,' his sister said. 'He sits there in that corner, scowling. Never has a word to say for himself from one week's end to the next.'

She was out of humour with the library. Sometimes people are little, hunched, overworked things, clamping over their working desks, grateful for mere kindness, she thought, looking at Sylvia as she downed her orange. And other times those same people at the same work desks are towering infernos, she felt, recalling Sylvia's ire the other day.

One of those silly rows, about nothing, so unexpected, out of the blue. One minute all had been normal, she had been talking, about some work thing, the next Sylvia had laughed

at her nastily, 'You're beginning to be a pest about that.' She
had burst into tears with astonishment: some factual matter
that she hadn't mentioned for days. Sylvia had been frightful,
at her computer, teeth clenched, seething with violence: 'I'll
walk out of here in a minute!'

...'My mother, my mother, my mother, my mother!' In his
squat, P fantacizes as he masturbates:

'It's a ruddy dream-world you've built for yourself!'

His sister, leaning over, her tit in his mouth, shouting at
him when she realizes he is the murderer sought by police.

'What do you want to do? Be a serial killer? Cross with
yourself because you've only killed one? All this... death and
disease and misery in the world, and you have to go round
killing people! Is it drama you want? Saying *I'm* your mother!
Trying to make yourself *interesting!*

'That's what you're at. Isn't it? Eh? Not using me, sister-is-
my-mother, as an excuse. O no! You *planned* this an as excuse
before. Read it somewhere! So as to make yourself interesting,
to God-damned *psychiatrists!* "Is he mad or is he bad or has he
been hurt?" Well I know you, boy. You ain't mad and you ain't
hurt! *Bad* is what you are!'

Now she stood far away, yelling at him. 'There's nothing
wrong with you! You've had no better or worse a life than
millions of others! Too much booze, *that's* for sure!'

She came to him, crying, 'O God, God, my God, how could
you have done it, O my God, P, what have you done!'

In the library, his sister, a thought prompted by her reading:
There is always a need to *lay the blame* for death. Not long after
her own husband's death, sharing a car with the man whose

wife had died of drink and Distalgesic, tight with terror as he began slapping the steering-wheel in venom, letting the car veer all over the road. 'I was just getting over it when this pal of mine at work – well I thought he was a pal – comes straight out with it, "O hadn't you thought of offering her organs for transplant, Jimmy?"'

No wonder people hate the bereaved. They're scared of saying something stupid. Often they do - but just as often the most innocuous thing can set them off because they have a need to lay the blame.

From the lavatory at his sister's P heard two old women in the lane outside.

'Ow's ye daughter?'

'Don't see 'e'.'

'O! O, I remember last time, you said you weren't seein' 'e'...'

'Don't see 'e'. Don't speak to 'e'.'

'Shame.'

'Broke me 'eart.'

'You bring 'em up, you do everything you can for them, they grow up, they don't appreciate what you've done for 'em. Some of 'em. My boy, O, he appreciates me!'

The other woman changed the subject, asking the first what she had bought for lunch.

He found himself recalling and growingly increasingly irate at the things they said: his sister's friend from the library, pontificating about... something to do with 'People are just the product of their environment ... or what's happened to them... or what has been done...' His sister had really put her down. They had been on about good and evil: is there a moment when you can say yea or nay?

These days he was overwrought, nervous, diarrhoeal, having to rush to the loo.

'Ah well,' that silly cow Sylvia had slavered, 'Like it says in the Psalms: Those who sow in tears will reap joy.'

Walking around the village. Walking towards him a tall slender girl in long flowing skirt, her face half-hidden by long flowing hair. Pulling her cuffs down to hide her hands.

...Walking around with her head down, cocked to one side, thinking she's fooling all the boys. Romantic twit! Swooning at her own supposed beauty! What's beautiful about that long thin face, you ignorant virgin!

...Two boys, the elder playing bucking bronco on his bike.

...The three most gorgeous looking kids. The parents always seemed angry, perhaps from the strains of rearing them: all three were very small. They were blonde, blue-eyed, minutely exquisite. There could be little more than a few months between them, and the eldest, a boy, was barely more than three. The parents' voices declaimed that they did not come from here, as did the names addressed to the two who toddled or walked in front of the push-chair, 'Charlotte, take Alexander's hand.' 'Well why didn't you tell me that half an hour ago!' he had heard the mother exclaim once when the eldest was on his way to nursery school, spinning the two youngest in the double-pushchair round and back into the house to pick up whatever he'd said he had to have for that morning's lesson. One Sunday the sight of the father with two or three golf-clubs over his shoulder - at first sight resembling gardening implements - prompted the thought that he was about to clout his tiny pink- coated daughter as he shepherded her into their drive.

A man was coming out of his garage, calling to his

neighbour, 'Have you got anything that tests whether the batteries are any good?'

'The thing I have got is...' P heard as he passed.

Sometimes an open garage revealed a countryman's pursuits: green wellies; a pair of waders; fishing-rods.

...What sort of a fiend has a sticker that reads *Ban Blood Sports* on the back of his car? Probably the sort who beats his wife and breaks the necks of his kiddies. He knew the bastard kept a dog who bit, for it had bitten him - fucking little terrier, one minute, no sign, the next it had been out here, fangs stuck into his leg. That was his car with green stickers all over it, parked all over the God-damned pavement, cut out of a naked woman, all boobs, in the back. He wished he had a set of keys: that way, he could scratch cars that parked across the pavement...

Stop the trade in ivory - you buy, they die he read on a car sticker. He could hear his sister, going on: 'What about the poor carvers? Their livelihood going down the swanee, for the sake of elephants that're already dead: burning good tusks..!'

So much pontificating from the back of cars... Always commands: do this, stop that, prevent the other.

Again he heard his sister's voice: 'Bad as America! Land of the free!' Why don't they just have done with it, he thought, and stick in their windows: Go fuck yourself; Up yours.

...Three women, hogging the pavement, gurgling and gargling over some little kid.

Late that night he got up and went to the fields, looking for the lovers in their car, but they didn't come.

The next morning, a letter arrived from the Job Centre calling him in for special interview.

Toytown music coming from an ad on the TV below. From the bathroom she thought she heard a door: the sound of her brother letting himself in.

P tried fantasizing terror from his sister's viewpoint; the brother as himself though not her brother, though a serial killer. He had read about one such the night before, in a paper he had found blowing across the fields: some cunt called Dahmer, who dismembered his victims. Took photos of them, too, just like that other joker, Neilson, did. What was this about homosexuals, forever 'boiling the heads to remove the flesh.' Old flat-foot going up to Neilson, 'A've come abhart your drains.' Sitting down to watch his sister's video, he laughed himself silly at the notion.

'Now that's not very nice, is it? Put it away, dear.' - Old woman on whom he had just pulled a knife in her home.

He wished that he could be alone, in his squat, self-sufficient, but the bungalow lacked electricity or running water. He could not shave, or boil a kettle, or flush a loo. He peed in the garden and squatted in the shrubbery behind the old greenhouse. One day he'd returned to his squat from his sister's. The garden had been cleared, a notice stuck up on the tree that planning permission was being sought for another bungalow in the garden. His ire rose as though he were the owner. Another bungalow! Here! Garden's too small.

They had not been in the bungalow, thinking it empty; no sign that they had even tried the door. Not even opened it to get post, although a pile of brown window envelopes, junk mail, bills, had gathered since he had been there. At first P had used the window but now he went in and out through the door. He felt like an enraged owner. A new bungalow! In my garden! They've let this bungalow go to rot!

The garden had been cleared. He had to find another place to pee and squat, behind a short hedge of Leylandii.

A family had moved into the empty bungalow opposite. This was a proper home, made of brick, a house rather than a bungalow since it had an upstairs dormer. An old lady had lived there till she'd died. Passing on his walks before he'd moved in, he had often seen her with her vile yappy dog, envisaged visiting grandchildren in those dormers.

He didn't know if there were any grandchildren, but her inheritors had certainly moved in, parking their Escort across his drive once, bloody great removals van filling the lane.

Theirs was a proper home: brick-built. Roses round the gate and trained along the garage; yuccas and hanging-baskets in the front porch.

Whereas all his house had was a busted main window, a busted garage door. That busted mauve door outside which Blowzy had parked her purple Chevvy seemed to epitomize his bungalow.

'Doesn't it look poignant!' one of the new people had cried of the half-coconut still hanging outside his broken window-pane.

The windows of his bungalow grew progressively dirtier. He had hung up a sack to break up most of the somewhat small plate-glass pane, flinging it up over a nail on days when he registered that the sun was particularly bright. Often he kept the sack hanging for days at a time. He did not like having people opposite – they might notice the difference, notice the sack going up and down, though in truth the thick, mainly rose hedge largely secluded the house at the far side of the lane.

He came often to his sister's, letting himself in when she was at work, squatting on the floor, his back to the sofa, or on the sofa, legs under him, dipping into crisps or chocolate chips and watching his videos.

The young woman with light pale-blue shorts atop her shapely thighs, cycling with her tiny son strapped in the child-seat behind her, his long but well-cut hair of purest white.

Turning the corner, in the lane, the tall man on the sit-up-and-beg, his strong face framed by an impossibly orange caricature of an Edwardian beard.

These his sister greeted as she passed. To him she railed, 'All the suffering in the world and you have to watch pornography... violence' – hurling across the room his video *The Silence of the Lambs.*

He had seen his sister one day say to Bill who was in a pate,

'Shall I compare thee to a summer's day?

Thou art more beauteous and more temperate.'

Bill had regained his temper, laughed, but P did not understand.

His sister was a very feminine woman. When she stood up out of a chair or walked into a room ahead of you, long ear-rings dangled either side of her dark hair, her curved hips swung. He always liked the warm creamy smell that wafted from her, as though she got her perfume out of a jar and rubbed it on, not one of these sickly-sweet too-spicy sprays. He always thought of her if ever he saw a film of Elizabeth Taylor: same height, same shape, same colour hair and eyes. The bosom, the hip designed to hoist a child...

'O you bad birds! Eating all the figs! Leave my figs alone! *Wicked* birds!'

He had come in just as his sister was exclaiming at the sight of half-eaten figs still hanging from the tree.

'Aye, you know which ones are ripe – you eat them before

they've fallen! He's going to have to net this!'

She had been planning to take some figs to one of her permanently-ill. He had heard her laughing once to Bill, 'I don't know what he does for it - you never even see him with a girlfriend!'

She made a noise, you heard her through the walls, crying out or calling, *'Bill, Bill!'*

Lying alone, it made him have fantasies of lying beside her, pressing his hot hard thrust against her soft warm buttocks.

Now on the couch he tossed himself off before the video, he thrust and threshed, moaning, complaining, crying out, his open mouth wet-wide against the cushion, relieving himself into an empty pot-noodle carton.

When he had done he got up and made himself a cheese and tomato sandwich. One of his peculiarities was that he never ate the outsides of tomatoes. 'Indulging his foibles,' his sister said whenever she saw him squeezing out the seeds onto lettuce or cheese or cress.

'Life's too short to eat the outside of tomatoes.'

He threw the tomatoes onto the compost and ate his sandwich watching the lunchtime news.

His sister ate her own lunch in the library, happy to man the desk while the others went out to celebrate someone's birthday. She had given up smoking to save money and now she had given up drinking because she didn't like drinking without smoking.

'These days I can't stand to watch a drunk even on television. I've suddenly realized the violence of it all - mainly of men towards women, but even of men towards themselves.'

She had had a father who drank, in moderation save at Christmas and perhaps one or two other times a year; he was not a drunkard, not an alcoholic; but what reached out to her now from her childhood and appalled afresh was the *uncertainty:* she and her mother treading on egg-shells; the drunk's merry Christmas demolished so quickly to quibble then rage: *how will it be?*

Her husband had drunk. Her father had called her husband a drunkard, though with him there had never seemed to be that terrified anticipation. She had sometimes hidden bottles from him – only of beer.

Funnily enough her father had insisted that she did drink when she was little; had refused, when she went to that Methodist Sunday school, to let her sign the pledge. 'I'm not having her signing this. She has to be able to learn to drink socially... be part of society...' the card torn up before her eyes.

Yes. The unpredictability of living with a drunken man. She would not stand for it now, from Bill or any of them.

She could do nothing about it with P.

She had given up smoking and drinking herself. On the other hand, you didn't want to be like those Americans, where everything was permitted except what offended someone, which meant that nothing was permitted. Land of the free indeed! Don't inflame the sexists or the racists; don't even use the word stud because it has connotations of gender: 'though how anything female is supposed to be able to father a child is beyond my comprehension.'

P was still at his sister's when Bill arrived: on the step, tickling the cat behind the ear, singing to it from *Postman Pat.* P heard him say to his sister, 'There's you quoting Shakespeare and with him it's Postman Pat!'

'Milkman Bill

'Milkman Bill

'Milkman Bill
'And his little ger-bil,'
he sang, tugging the cat's whiskers.
'Are you postman Pat's black and white cat?
'Eh?'
His sister was indoors, preparing a salad; her friend from
the library in front of the television. From the lounge the
television chanted,
'Don't pay through the nose,
'Just go straight to Rumbalows...'
P saw his sister laughing, clutching her sides. She stood
in the doorway, 'O! O God. What have we come to. "Shall I
compare thee to a summer's day?" Four and a half centuries
later: "Don't pay through the nose, just come straight to
Rumbalows." Imagine that copywriter, going home, "Hey,
love, I came up with a good one today!"'
It had become a joke between her and Bill: "'Shall I compare
thee to a summer's day?" "O, I shouldn't bother if I were you."'
P sat on the steps, one minute singing 'Postman Pat' to the
cat, the next rubbing its hair up the wrong way with increasing
ferocity until in the end pulling its whiskers.
At the sound of the scream his sister raced out, pulling the
cat from his grasp.
'You can't do anything right! You can't even stroke a cat!
And why? Because half the time you're drunk out of your tiny
mind!'
Her friend had run out at the commotion and Bill had made
an appearance though he had pretended he had only looked
into the kitchen to get a drink.
When they had dispersed P sat on the step alone, without
even the cat. Some vulgar verse about behind the woodshed...

pulling my pud ran constantly through his mind. There was a woodshed at his sister's: delapidated, the putty falling from the windows. He had visions of scrambling into the privacy behind it, amongst briars and nettles doing vile things.

Since his suspicion that Bill would propose, P had grown violent towards his sister. His effing and blinding led to more rows.

She came across pornography in the bedroom.

'Not in my house!'

Bill said, 'It's normal enough in a boy of that age...'

'*That's* not normal! Have you seen them? Bestiality, sado-masochism,' flinging the magazines down in front of him. '*That's* not normal!

'Take these back to your own place, your *squat,* whatever! Don't leave this *filth* in my *house!*' Picking up magazines, scrunching in fury, she hurled them at P and stormed out.

She walked the August streets, her bosom heaving. It was too hot to have rows. 'It's one thing when it's grown men and women! There's men with animals, men with children!'

Leaving that *filth at her house!*

He pretended to still live at home with her. That way he got some sort of rental allowance paid. He paid no rent where he stayed – some sort of squat. The difference she supposed he spent at the pub.

Still agitated, she walked, trembling, with the dog, pondering the nature of evil. If someone killed Bill, would I forgive? Privately, she was worried about P - about how much evil there was in him. Was there evil in him? Was there evil in anyone? Was not all down to the genes and the biography?

Her thoughts scattered as two giant dogs bounded against the wire of their compound, barking at full volume, hurling themselves with vast leaps against the wire with great ferocity.

Her dog pulled towards them. She yanked it back, trembling at the violence of her shock and the violence of her own reaction.

There's your answer. Those dogs are meant to guard, but they're also there to intimidate. I love and know dogs, but even I am trembling. What would the sound and sight of two oversized slavering alsatians do to a child? By God, if a pit-bull attacked even P I'd want its owner's guts for garters. I would. God knows how I'd feel if some dog, let alone some man, had attacked my child.

She was still yanking her dog back, full rein, from the scene of great uproar and violence.

After its run she took the dog back by the roadway so as to avoid the alsatians. She passed the spot where, last year, a peacock had been trotting across the road.

Everybody loves the sight of a peacock. Stick a peacock in the middle of the road, holding up the traffic, and it is the one thing that makes every driver laugh: its huge feet, so much like hands, deliberately placed one before the other as it takes its time to cross.

Last year you couldn't pass this spot without seeing the peacock.

Last year the peacock flew.

This year there is no peacock.

Chapter 10

There they were, cutting a swathe through the field, and she felt as though she had cut a swathe through a field: as though she had broken through to some more hopeful time.

She remembered the planting of the winter corn last year: the return of hope, after all that hard work and the depression of deaths: her father's and the memories it had revived of her child's and her husband's, only to be followed by this year's list of fires, disappointments, illnesses, bereavements. Now here was that same corn being harvested.

Hares scattered from the centre of the field, scattering in their turn a flock of birds; the birds took to the trees above them. The ground was not level, its uneven sheen adding to its charm: the grey-green of the low humps and hillocks of the newly-ploughed fields of autumn sprung by November into uneven tufts of green, rising in spring into this great swaying mass of golden August.

She seemed to have had some row with her friend from the library, P thought, for the old bat regularly disagreed with her these days.

'Tender loving care is all that most people want,' the friend had argued.

'Ah, yes. Trouble is, you have to give it as well as take...'

'Sometimes the trouble is that some people even have trouble taking it...'

Bill had said, with a wink, 'Getting more right-wing in her old age.'

...'That freebie is pushed through your door every week with obsolete Marxist-Leninist ideals applied to a British situation, and filth untold in its editorials: "Which leg your willie's lying on" indeed! And this comes through the door, for kiddies to pick up and read. And you can't stop this – no Advertising Authority – the newspaper boy picks up his bag and he's told, "Deliver this to every home."'

Sometimes she laughed at it: "'Democracy has been tried nowhere." It's a wonder he isn't saying, "Communism hasn't been tried."

'These God-damned sentimentalists who eulogize communism and Utopia and eighteenth-century Enlightenment!' she laughed. 'People aren't born good! It's logical: we're born helpless, knowing only our own wants, hence we're born selfish. If we emerged fully-formed out of some sort of shell you could argue about innate good, innate bad; as it is, *logic* decrees that, as we're born knowing only our own needs, we have to be taught the needs and rights of others.'

The cold sink of the heart of the 19th of August; the surprised lift of the heart at the news that Yeltsin had climbed aboard a Russian tank. 'Well this one won't last,' she had told Bill.

After the coup had failed she'd said, 'What did they think would happen? China was the bottom line. Put up or shut up: kill your own people in the streets or let them live the way they like. Ironical, isn't it – *China's* behind all these revolutions.'

She added, of Russia, 'They needed that. Now they feel like everybody else. Another coup be blowed – there won't be another coup! In *Russia!*'

Sylvia had invited her to attend some lecture at the library for the local writers' circle. Abhorring the waste of a summer's evening, duty decreed that she take this olive-branch.

Youngish don in open-necked shirt, seemingly the coolest one here, pleased with himself at having brought out his first thriller: no one had ever done that before. She sat, trying to fan herself with her neck-line while the audience of mainly middle-aged women of Sylvia's persuasion were waiting only to hear how they themselves could get published and to have him read and uncritically praise their work.

He paced the stage, a bit of a Jonathan Miller: legs long, arms wide, fingers pointing, gracing the lectern only to check his next cue.

'In one word I can tell you what art is. Art is *industry*. But people don't like that. It's not romantic. It's not *airy-fairy* enough. It's not *arty-farty*.

'To get *bums on seats* you need *bums on seats*. In other words, some idiot has to sit down and write the words before some other idiot can act it or play it or perform it and other *people* can *pay* them for *doing so.*'

She was walking in the road so as to pass an approaching family of Indians. She wanted to be noticed.

Her carriage was exquisite. At first he'd thought she was the half-American woman who lived next door to his sister: tall, erect, hair up ...Austrian... mid-European.

She wore a mauve silk blouse, almost sleeveless, tucked into the tight waist of black slinky trousers, silk-like themselves and with a vast pattern of ferns, flowers or trees. She walked with an elegance, long ear-drops tinkling. From the top of her low-bunned hair to the click of her patent heels, she was exquisite.

Her bum was too big for her waist, he thought. Perhaps it was the cut of her trousers. Terribly tight waist.

She carried an elegant straw bag with something written on it. He couldn't see what. Maker's name. No tat.

She turned into a side-street. With a swagger. That bitch. Knows what she is. Deserves to be followed. Asking for it.

Deserves to be done in. He turned the corner after her.

Gat-teeth, she thought. Must tell the police... gat-teeth...

Packing his Polaroid, he left the flat. Bottom too big. Deserved to be killed.

The big combine with its cloud of dust and sickening-sweet smell of new-mown hay.

Perhaps it was the combine that stank. Did they have catalytic converters? A combine on unleaded petrol? Maybe that's why it was green.

It stank so much and made such noise that, even at this distance, he had no desire to go near it. So much for the peace of the country.

On the way home he saw in someone's garden a tin labelled FLOUR, full of flowers, which made him laugh.

'...Angst never created anything. It's no good being so full of *angst* you feel a *failure* before you *start*. You have to do it...'

She left the lecture-hall singing to herself under her breath Glenn Gould's *So You Want to Write a Fugue:*

'Get up and do it,

Just do it,

Just do it,

Do it,

Do it.'

Breathing the fresh night air she sang out loud,
'What is more you will conclude
 That Sebastian Bach
 Was a very clever charp...'

Chapter 11

Summer seemed to have ended swiftly this year. By the end of August the mist of the morning returned before seven for evenings in a row. In London, where Bill drove down for business one or two days a week, the streets around Marylebone retained some of the lightness and heat at ten in the evening that he remembered from when he'd lived round here in that blazing hot summer of '76, but in the country the nights drew cold before dark.

Sometimes P's sister encouraged him to go with Bill to London. 'At least it'll get you away from moping round the house.'

Crossing the road, P saw a sticker in a rear side view window, facing out. He read it, expecting to see *Children should be seen and not hurt* or *Keep death off the roads – don't wear fur,* but this one read, in block caps, **BORN TO SHOP.**

He walked away feeling disgusted, having no words to put round his disgust. Born to love, born to hate, born to do anything that's human, born to birth, born to kill, but *born to shop!*

Presumably some man had put it there for his wife. Presumably they'd thought it was a hilarious joke.

How could they?

Without shame or embarrassment?

Had they no *shame?*

The whole of life reduced to born to shop.

P had no words to put round any of this. He walked on, disgusted, feeling filthy, shat upon, murderous, obscene.

...and style. Undressing her, he had seen the labels. She had dressed from the local chain- store and it looked like she had dressed from Dior.

After he'd killed her he had picked up the bag only to read the boring logo: **MY BAG.**

The next day he had walked again amongst the heavily-mown fields. A brilliant August harvest day; Hollywood could do no more: whole sheared fields shining beneath blue skies of warm but not hot, bright but not blinding sun. Most fields were harvested, one, duller, bearing still its corn; some with corn gathered; some bearing baled straw.

The sight and dull sound of a thresher being worked at the mouth of a distant barn (perhaps separating the wheat from the chaff on that small patch of field kept every year different, apart, from the others: farmed organically, perhaps, or grown by a child? - This corn was never stacked but lay in clumps, perhaps cut by hand.)

Swinging brown arms. The golden-brown of a field of new-mown hay beneath the sun.

Swinging no more. He had chopped her up and shoved the pieces in **MY BAG.**

He had removed the ear-rings and put them in his pocket where they jangled while he walked.

He entered his sister's to hear her with that old bat from the library, going on about evening classes.

'...£500 a year.'

'A *term*.'

'A *term?*'

Seeing him, his sister said, 'What's these?'

Holding out the ear-rings.

He snatched them and left, hearing her tell the old crone, '...turning out his jeans' pocket...'

'Well you always do, don't you, every pocket, before you stack that washing-machine...'

...Sucking the ear-ring, rousing himself, until he pulled the pants off her and took her.

She was dry.

She was dead.

There was blood on her.

Congealed blood lay thick on her white neck.

He took her still.

O, what a beauty!

Her features motionless in death.

For he was fierce and hot and alive; what came out of him was fierce and hot and living.

Chapter 12

She was dabbing herself with Elizabeth Taylor's *Passion* prior to going out somewhere with Bill.

...She looked a million dollars. I chopped that million dollars into a million pieces!

Walking with the dog, he was passed by a boy riding his bike, standing on his peddles, his bum high out of the saddle, yelling what sounded like, 'Mum, I've found another nurstrum!' He cycled amongst his friends, saying excitedly, 'There's a mushroom on our lawn!'

P could hear his sister, 'What's the matter with kids now? You can't hear a word they're saying half the time.

...'If you don't draw the line for kids someone else is going to draw it for them. At every age, you draw the line, they step over it, but they know that there is a line, they know they daren't step too far: that is what discipline, that is what *bringing up* is.

'You don't get kids *brought up* any more. They're given birth to and left to fend – over-indulged or under-disciplined half the time, with parents divorced, without fathers. Well you can't tell me this is normal! No wonder there's rioting on the streets, on housing estates. And you can't tell me all this is poverty and unemployment – my father, our fathers, they left school at fourteen, they worked to support brothers and sisters and widowed mothers, on an apprentice's pay, *they* didn't have dole cheques or youth clubs but *they* didn't go on the rampage. No, I won't have it, I'm not accepting that. This is devilment for the sheer hell of it. We don't tell kids no, we don't draw the line, we don't teach them right from wrong any more.

Racing around some housing estate in stolen cars, stabbing a woman who goes out to remonstrate – stabbing a woman outside her own door. Terrorizing people, that's all they're doing. Boredom be jiggered. It's pure neat sadism.

'If you don't draw the line for kids someone else is going to draw it for them, and some of them are going to have it drawn around their necks.'

Chapter 13

The hawthorn bore their berries now. Wild blackberries grew in profusion along the field path.

She made a 'phone call to Alec's wife and talked to Alec. They had been on two weeks' holiday at his mother's caravan in North Norfolk. He said he had been active, taking part in the kids' games. 'I even drove part of the way home. I enjoy driving - it relaxes me.' He had been fishing with a friend and brought home three trout. He said that he felt well, was in no pain. 'Though I must admit it was a heck of a shock at first to find I'd got this illness.' He talked of visiting friends at work, the collapse of the Russian class, Russia in general, concern for Bertha, of whose fire he had heard.

They cut the excess growth off the fig tree so that the post-woman could get to the front door. The figs this year were moist and not over-sweet. The year before they had tasted of Nutrasweet.

Throwing onto the heap the bird-eaten figs, cutting off the leaves, milk falling from the branches, the leaves themselves were huge, grotesque, their own particular heavily-veined green.

'I love that fig tree. I wouldn't be without that fig tree. There's nothing like a fig tree for sheer vulgarity.'

After that they netted it, he climbing up the ladder, his sister handing up to him the netting and the ties.

He gathered up his prunings. Giant leaves, some a foot long, so thick as to be leathery, each phallic triad grotesquely enlarged, dripping its white milk onto his gardening shoes.

They went in for their meal and went out after and finished

their task in the early September dark. He stood at the compost heap as the church clock struck eight.

'How can anyone doubt the existence of God when they look at a fig tree?' his sister laughed. 'There has to be a grand design behind *that*.'

A day or so after the netting, he held up his sister to reach a newly-ripened fig. She retrieved it from between the layers of net, laughing girlishly, 'O the things we do! Here, this one's yours; you deserve this!'

Climbing into bed that night, she said to Bill, 'You know what I could eat?'

He gestured query with his upturned hands as he prepared to clamber into bed.

'The Marks & Sparks prawn sandwich longer than which the pair of Ratner ear-rings do not last.'

He laughed. 'The prawn sandwich that passeth.'

'Not as fast as the fig that passeth.'

Everything was coming to fruition at once: fig, plum-tree, apple. Once every week she prepared stewed fruit and sponge. Bill collected fallen apples from the two trees old as the century, lacking a ladder high enough for their tops.

She stood at the sink, singing:

'I'll pick some apples in autumn a-gain

And cook the buggers in an Eng-lish lane

And chase the maggots down the sink a-gain...'

Bill was laughing.

She said to him, 'Look at this! He's been doing the breast-stroke. I put the knife in to wash the gunge off: where's that beetle? He's half-way up my sink! They're not ear-wigs, they're coddling-moths. That's what you get inside the apple. I'm lucky if I can use a quarter of each.'

'You should have seen the ones I threw away.'

Listening to a radio report of how the surviving coup members were being held in jail until their trial, although, for security reasons, the guards had been changed, she began singing, 'They're changing guards at the Lubyanka...'

She turned at a knock at the door to see the police.

Chapter 14

Two young joyriders had been killed when the stolen car they were driving had hit a lamp-post and burst into flames. 'No doubt their parents will say it's the fault of the man who had his car stolen for buying such a powerful model in the first place.'

Bill said of her half-amusedly, 'She's a chatterbox but she's got a good heart.'

The joyriders blamed police for the deaths. In the next few nights, riots ensued. Clergymen claimed the joyriders were disadvantaged.

'When do these cunts imitate Christ in the temple? They're so busy turning the other cheek to evil they forget about overturning the tables of the moneylenders.'

Sir John Gielgud's Bible reading was about to start: the first 13 episodes from Genesis. She found herself tuning in to *The Daily Service* to try to find longwave Radio 4. To her astonishment a lot of the services nowadays were conducted by women. Had she heard aright? Was God the Father *she?*

'Of course God the Father is male. All this business about God the mother! The Bible's full of it. "Praise me! Praise me constantly! Praise the Lord!" All men want constant praise. Women just get used to getting on with it, day by day.'

And after that was *Woman's Hour,* if she let it run on because the cat was on her knee, calling some woman a *Chair!*

'Why not President for Chair?' Bill suggested.

'O, but that's *thinkism.* You're not allowed to *think* because that's not *fair,* what about the ones with a lower IQ? Can't wait for the day when the *differently abled* Aids victim rapes the disadvantaged black lesbian. Whose side will they dare to come down on then?'

Bill laughed as she switched off the set and put the cat down. 'And I thought PC meant your word processor!'

The day after the police had called round, wrongly, it turned out, about someone else's parked car, the greengrocer had stopped her just as she was on her way to catch a bus to tell her that Alec was ill again.

'It's a tragedy. A family man, a community man. A good sort.'

The news cast her down. She would have to tell Elaine. ...Stopping her bike to talk when they'd first known: 'I mean, he was just a nice guy... He is a nice guy...' ...In those cold January days, the February snows, stopping her bike to talk, fearful for her son: 'I mean, it doesn't matter how good a soldier you are, with chemical weapons...'

This year had never recovered from its start with the Gulf War...The church's comments on the rioting in Oxford and Newcastle; news of the death of an old school friend; the re-assertion of Alec's illness; the cancer of the woman two doors from Bertha; the death of the husband of the woman with the alsatian, followed within the week by the death of her mother...

'He's got a nerve! The Church of England – talking about illiteracy as one of the causes of riot, after what his lot have done to the liturgy! There's my father, left school at fourteen. On his deathbed he said, "If God's ever given man owt better than poetry, 'e's never shown it to me." He sat, as a choir-boy, through reading after reading from the *Authorized* Version, the *King James'* Bible.

'The church used to give people literature, music and art. Now it's all *Good News* Bible in modern English which is, incidentally, not even faithful to the Greek, for all their claims; there's *pop music* before the pulpit, and all *join in* and *shake hands.* The Church has become farcical. It gives people nothing. Liberality does nothing but hurt people. Kids need a line. As for unemployment, poverty being the cause of riots – there's a woman been beaten up outside her own house, for going outside, remonstrating. Not a word of disapprobation! The *victim* gets it in the neck these days!'

Chapter 15

'Why wasn't she reported earlier?'

'Well she wasn't from round here, you see. Nobody knew she was missing. She'd gone to stay at her friend's, at this empty flat. Her friend found her when she got back. She's only just got back from holiday.'

P heard this with contempt. It wasn't a flat but a bungalow. Why couldn't they get their facts right?

The woman had walked into the bungalow next to his own, so far away and so deeply screened that he had never seen it before.

He had simply followed her through the gate.

...'O her poor friend! Fancy finding that! Her body must have been in a dreadful state...'

'O it wasn't,' P interrupted brightly. 'It was cut up. Whoever killed her cut her up!'

'Cut her up!'

'O how terrible!'

'Must have been a butcher. I mean, to cut someone up, you need weapons...'

His tale spread, became embroidered: 'She found her friend's head propped up on the sofa. No body under. Just lolling, propped up by pillows.'

The police had already interviewed him once, as a neighbour, asking if he had seen anything. Where had he been, as a matter of interest? Probably, he had thought, at his sister's. His sister too thought this likely. 'He's always in and out of here.'

'Are you likely to find him, whoever did it?'

'Delay's the problem. Same problem everywhere. No one

can exactly remember where they were, what they were doing.'

O but they must remember her! That silky mauve top! That great beauty! He tossed in the night, repeating, 'O but they must remember her!'

He had followed her to the bungalow. He had knocked on the door, introducing himself as a neighbour, called round for some sugar.

Indoors, she had looked in the strange cupboards. 'I think she keeps her sugar here...'

'I like something sweet,' he had said, moving his hands behind her.

'Yes, you must remember that night!' Sylvia said to her. 'You weren't in! That was the night of the lecture! You must remember...'

'O yes...'

Her fears had been quenched at first when she'd heard that the woman was 'cut up' and after he'd said he had found the earrings.

'Well he did have a pair of ear-rings but there was no blood on his clothes, no blood at all. I washed his jeans – that's how I found the ear-rings. I thought they were mine at first...'

'He's off his head. She's in one piece. He didn't cut her up at all. There is a slight mark at the neck, where he seems to have tried to stick a small vegetable knife in after he'd strangled her.

'Not very efficient, the killer - there was a Cretan knife in the drawer, right next to where it happened.'

That wasn't it I didn't mean it that wasn't real. It wasn't even fun

P thought to himself as he was bodily carted away by police, strong-armed backwards, out of his squat into the car that filled the narrow lane.

'Why do you kill people?'
Why did he kill people! *Huh!*
Because they had homes and lights in windows and people around them and purple Chevvies and mauve garage-doors.

When he was charged, P felt, No, no, you don't understand. *Born to shop – that's* disgusting.
Murder is crisp, cold, sharp, *clean.*
Better that we should all be murdered than live in the sewer *born to shop.*

There's nobody in the world who sees me as a human being Including me.

For days she had been plagued by lines of Byron running through her head:
...and strangled her.
No pain felt she.
I am quite sure
She felt no pain.
'That poor girl's terror. He's my brother, but I can't stop...'
She was shuddering, imagining again as she had ceaselessly since the news broke the petrified moment when that girl realized what she must suffer at the hands of this man, *my brother.*

Despite the sun, despite the heat, a lot of blackberries had not ripened this year.

'I mean, he was ever so good when he was helping me net that fig.'

She stopped, for he had already done the murder when he had helped her with the fig.

The fig tree stood, still netted, its leaves brown and withered, pendulous rotten figs.

She burst out crying, 'We might just as well have left them to the birds!'

At the compost heap at his squat she said tearfully, 'You hardly need forensics round here. That's the way he throws out tomatoes. I've never known anyone else who throws away tomatoes like that.'

He could hear the voices of the village women, telling his sister, 'You'll stand by him. I know you'll stand by him.'

He could hear his sister's voice, feel her clout him across the head:

'Psychopath! He's not a psychopath! He's not even sufficiently unformed to be a psychopath!

'Getting your ideas from these American TV programmes, all out to make money out of you!'

Turning to some woman friend, 'I mean, he wanted to be a *serial killer!* I ask you!'

The *shock* of realizing that it's not a game. *Before* and *after.* One chance. The way his sister was always rabbiting on about weddings:

'The trouble is, it's so easy the first time. Anyone can do it.

Anyone can get married *once*. You're free. You don't realize what giving up your freedom means till it goes wrong. Then you realize what being trapped means.'

P was found hanging in his cell.

She wrote to the press:

My brother was naïve for his age, but he was only 19 when he hanged himself. He was not given a chance to grow up. I am a librarian and no one is more aware than I of the need to preserve freedom of speech. I am very aware that people will say, no one was ever driven to commit murder or rape by watching videos; the evil or imbalance must be in them already for such imitation to be triggered. Be this as it may, are we prepared to allow susceptible youngsters to be so triggered?

My brother committed a crime and he paid the price – the most grave of crimes and the highest price. For God's sake let us look at this system again, look at what we are allowing our young people to watch every day on television, to watch repeatedly on video, for the balance now is surely not right... and because of this we have lost two unique human lives.

The ground, cleared in mid-summer, was again overgrown. They had stuck a *For Sale* sign on P's squat. A second letter demanding that he attend for interview or risk forfeiting his dole arrived after his death.

She pulled the dog back from the bushes, returning with him to the quiet road. She had dreaded losing Bill this year. Instead it had been P that she had lost.

She took the dog across the fields, returning home along the narrow path, waving her arms wildly as bluebottles swarmed up from the dead plums.

Part 2

DAY OF ATONEMENT

John 11:25 KJV: Jesus said unto her, *I am the resurrection, and the life:* he that believeth in me, though he were dead, yet shall he live.

Chapter 16

A big dry brown sycamore leaf, held erect by the wind, its points touching the tarmac, tippy-tappy, tippy-tappy, like a hurrying woman in high-heels.

Patrick pulled her forward. It had begun to rain.

Still raining as she turned into her lane, finding herself behind a slow-walking young man hunched into his anorak. Living in a quiet lane, one so often saw youngsters walk down here, slowly, reluctantly, head-down, or sitting defeatedly on the low wall or on the potholed lane itself, leaning against a cottage, gnawing on their hurt rebellion or focused frustration following some failure, rebuff, or family argument.

She turned on the radio to hear the singing of 'How sweet the name of Jesus sounds/ In a believer's ear.'

The name Jesus always struck her as divisive. It means one thing to Catholics, another to Protestants, then there's the Arabs, the Jews.

News had arrived through the post of the death, 15 years ago, of an old school friend. She felt haunted by this, on top of her previous troubles - a revival it seemed of cancers in the village - the woman with the alsatian, losing her husband from cancer and then her mother in one week; even Elaine, despite her new healthy grandson, admitting, 'It is hard to keep your chin up this year.'

The preacher in the daily service, the tail-end of which she caught whilst waiting for the start of *Exodus,* more like a sociologist than a preacher, communist to boot: Was the feeding of the 5,000 a miracle or were all fed because the selfish stopped being greedy? She felt demeaned by religion:

as though the soul is housed in a cardboard box or a mansion, as though heaven will be ours if we could only take, forcibly, from the rich and give to the poor. Religion without hope, without spirit, religion without care, cherishment, charity.

Seeing David in the lane that same morning. Asking after his holiday, his grandchildren; the new evening classes; does he see Alec? He sees Alec every day; he was so-so yesterday.

'They're very positive, as a family, they have a very positive attitude, they mean to fight it together, and that's good; but I can't get them to see or to admit to any strength outside which could help them.' She nodded, recalling that he was a preacher, speaking of her own husband's death.

'Was that from cancer?'

His own son had died from a melanoma when he was thirty-three. 'This time of the year: autumn. When we found out. He went back to work. He had chemotherapy, what they could give him, then he went back to work. He was back at work, but he got progressively worse, he lingered, for six months: this time of the year, till February... snow... No one has ever survived a melanoma. Fortunately neither he nor I knew that at the time. I know it may sound a meaningless cliché, I'm not saying I'd choose a slow, painful death, but I'd had my span, his life was half-lived; I would have chosen that I could go in place of him.'

He turned the talk again back to Alec. She saw that he needed to minister unto him. From the family's viewpoint, they might be humanists, committed to living each day as it comes. She too had been talking of his quality of life, with his children, then saw that his thoughts ran in a deeper vein.

'I've conducted a lot of funerals, I had two churches, in

Jamaica, I was minister there to two parishes... a wooden church, up the hill. How often I've stood there, and spoken these words from John, at the gate to the cemetery, as the funeral cortege passed by. "I am the resurrection and the life..." Said them many times, at many funerals. And all at once, this day, suddenly, for no reason, I was saying these words and the words themselves struck me: here is a man saying that he is an *event...*'

The burning revelation of this made him stumble, his conversation jumped from his experience at the cemetery gates to recalling it later to seminary students. She saw that he gazed at her almost in grief: the grief of man's inability to convey deep thoughts one to the other; wondering: should I have spoken? Will I be mocked?

She did not mock. Integrity shone staunchly through his grief. A parson who will speak of soul, of man's inadequacy, of God; a minister who will minister.

He had not conveyed, for she could not take Christ as he did. Rather, perhaps, he had conveyed; he had not converted. He had conveyed. O! He had conveyed! The depths of a soul, laid bare, one man's view of heaven, one man's belief.

Of *Heaven!* Not of souls out of cardboard boxes, not of salvation out of a paper bag: a packet of sandwiches to the poor, a soup-run. A man who saw life as a soul's route to God: God's view of life; God's will: so that Ruth's death was not a cruelly foreshortened life but a calling of a soul to God; Alec's illness not a daily struggle to stay alive with his family, rollicking with his kids, but a trial for his soul, that it might meet its God.

O how hard is it to see God's will, to see it, let alone believe, to comprehend, let alone believe that it should be so. Man's view diametrically opposed to God's. Yet we pray it: *Thy will be done.*

Thy will be done.

Chapter 17

Liz Taylor had just married for the eighth time. Picking up the mink-edged purple pochette containing the last of the perfume bought for her in Beverly Hills, she could hear her brother's laughter, 'Mrs Fortensky's Passion!'

She swung between recalling Ruth and being lost in her grief for P.

The picture of Ruth's mother in the paper, launching her child-leukaemia appeal, looking so much like her own mother, the Jewishness subservient to the Yorkshire: the hairstyle, the clothes, the glasses. In fact she'd thought it was Ruth herself, a woman her own age, wry in the face of grief. But Ruth died fifteen years ago.

She felt cast back to those days when she and Ruth had been schoolgirls together, revising for their GCEs.

...She pretended always to be experienced. Standing aside for me: 'Ladies first.' We were both 15. It was all bluster. The girls always called her a silly dreamer: running away from home. She beat me to the Eng. Lit. prize, I know that. Dead. At 30. My God.

With grief still sharp for P, she had the recurrent feeling of the sadness of death at 30, the responsibility on those alive to grasp all life's opportunities.

...I'll bet she did not go gently into that good night. She always was a life-liver. No time to make her mark on the world: in her career, to marry, have a child. The all-singing, all-dancing, high-kicking Ruth. Her life full of drama. No drama now.

She thought Ruth had had talent locked in her that she

had no time to show, no time to develop, no time for luck to change; no time for the breaks; for maturity to bring new depths to her acting, for better parts. The fame she felt could have been hers denied her, by early death. All the frustrations of failure enveloped by the ultimate frustration of all. Death before one's full time. And *to see it coming.*

That was what Alec had to contend with, of course. But at least he had a family, a wife...

News of Ruth's death had made her feel old. She looked anew on mortality. 'My God, from now on we're going to celebrate every birthday,' she said to Bill. 'It might be the last!'

...Cast back to expostulating to P, 'What's the matter with you young these days? When I was young life was strong and sweet. Where's your youth? Where's your vitality? You drown it all in booze and drugs and watching that box. A young man has the world at his feet! He can do anything! I'm twice your age, and I've got ten times your oomph, your get up and go...'

She was haunted by thoughts of Ruth, dead these fifteen years, recalling what her own life would have lacked had she died at so early an age: no Stan, no little Polly, no Bill.

To die at 30: why, you hadn't begun. Especially in that profession.

Chapter 18

She had seen David setting off the next morning to make notes for his sermon on a day-long walk to the local stately home, 'to see autumn colour,' and had caught sight of him from the bus, returning, striding with his small rucksack over the brow of a hill.

She had still not found his Bible reference, *I am the resurrection & the life*, though she had read the whole of John. Was it 14,6: 'Jesus saith unto him, I am the way, the truth and the life: no man cometh unto the Father but by me.' She had also marked John: 8,12: 'Then spake Jesus again unto them, saying, I am the light of the world: he that followeth me shall not walk in darkness but shall have the light of life.'

Verily, verily, I say unto thee, When thou wast young, thou girdest thyself, and walkedst whither thou wouldest: but when thou shalt be old, thou shalt stretch forth thy hands, and another shall gird thee and carry thee withcr thou wouldest not.

One year on, another November, and here she was, equally cast down, equally pricked by the truth of John: 21, 18: as though she were already an old woman, as she walked Patrick across the fields.

She could get to P's truth but shakily: unreal still it felt; without a trial... curtailed.

She could get no closer to the woman's agony. They had found out little about her. She had been from abroad: an Austrian woman, over here on holiday.

'I can't believe he's dead. I still expect him to walk in through that door.'

She had written to Ruth's mother, enclosing something for her charity.

The wild hedging was still green with ivy, some small-leaved creeper, and that clematis that bore fluffy tufts (like the shaggy-haired sheep-dog who sometimes used this path), though the hedge at the side of the field, in summer a mass of dog-roses, was nothing but bare sticks, the orchard bare within.

Dry rye grass white and bright under the sunset.

The new corn sprouting green.

Some days the birds would chase each other in flocks; on other days, lone birds, fighting against the wind, tucked their wings into their bodies, blown sideways like sycamore seeds.

Some days noisy birds, rooks, crows; sometimes gulls, swooping; sometimes a cawing chatter, like rusty machinery, whilst other, small, birds twittered from the orchard, despite its being November.

On a mid-afternoon when the sunset was meagre: a lone gull, flying low over the November green fields so that he looked like a low-flying aircraft until he swooped up over a hedge in the distance the way no aircraft ever can.

She rang Alec herself now. He seemed much better. He had had some problem with jaundice: 'The bile salts make the skin itch and keep him awake, but the doctor has given him something for this.'

He was back to eating almost a normal diet. Red meat was too heavy for his digestion, but he could eat fish, chicken, low fat foods, lots of liquids, basically a health-conscious diet.

He had had various diagnostic scans and X-ray scans –

'magnetic resonance scanners.' The man responsible for his X-rays was very interested in his case. ('This is hardly surprising,' she told Bill later. 'He was given 3 months to live 9 months ago.')

He was waiting for a further appointment for a new scan - she heard his wife in the background say 'Nuclear...'

He was also still having acupuncture.

'What's that like?' she asked him.

'I can tell you just what it's like: it's like having a hair pulled. Sometimes you feel it but other times you don't feel anything. She always starts off by putting a few needles in the ears - to make you relax. Often I nearly fall asleep when she's doing it. It is very tiring.'

'His wife drives him there,' she told Bill later, 'but this Friday they're going to Cambridge to make a start on their Christmas shopping.' – 'Smashing not to have to do this at the weekend,' he had said.

She had found him very easy to talk to. No treading on eggshells, watching words. 'I felt confident about mentioning Christmas. He seems to be living, if not long-term, then medium-term - whereas before it was "day by day... one day at a time."

'No wonder he's become "an interesting case" to a scientist: as short a time as a few weeks ago, at half-term, we were talking about him as though this was the last holiday he would ever see with his children. Now he's talking about keeping up his Russian.'

It seemed that P had died but Alec would live.

...I could not give him the love or attention he needed... but I was so down myself... Then there was Bill... He was not very good at death; but foolish is the man in this world who does not take sympathy where he can get it.

She walked across fields with the dog every spare hour till the afternoons grew dark and the winds grew cold, till her eyes smarted with tears she knew not from grief or the cold cutting rain.

As she turned off the field path into the road, towards where the lit houses marked the start of the village, pulling the dog onto the grass bank out of the path of a passing car, the voice of her brother, half-playful, half-mocking, 'Nance, the lance, can prance,' invaded her thoughts.

Chapter 19

By a certain evening light the tall dead rye-grass looked as golden as summer corn.

December drew on, the man-high gorse in the deep dusk resembling a man; white as stiff snow upon an icy dawn.

On frost-covered pavements she passed the yucca, planted outside on account of its great height. Its long leaves hung limp, its top tied with cement-bag. That was the house where the dog had died of cancer. The yucca itself was a gift to his mother from an RAF pilot, its longevity tentatively symbolizing to her her son's own good health.

The tall grass and gorse was white now with bristling hoar-frost, sparkling like Christmas tinsel.

Returning with Patrick through the frosted streets, the sound of *God Rest Ye Merry, Gentlemen* being played on a clarinet rang through an upstairs window – strange that it should be wide on so frosty a morn. Perhaps he was showing off, for he played well.

The sight of adverts for Christmas shows – *Toad of Toad Hall;* the village panto - stuck in the ground or pasted on a wall, redoubled her isolation from the normal life that went on around her. She was sending no Christmas greetings this year.

She took the dog for a walk by a different route, past where the *Pig & Ferret* was being re-built. There was talk of the Prime Minister attending the re-opening next week. They had run the restaurant side from their home since the fire; she and Bill had once seen four guests arriving: strangers in full evening dress going into a private house to pay for a meal cooked by a chef with his own radio programme, famous too for his television shows. They had talked of taking P once for Christmas dinner.

She was still listening to the Bible readings. 'O no, it's the King James' Version!' she had told David in October. Until the New Testament – I shan't listen to that. She had kept a piece from *The Times:* Rabbi Friedlander, of the Day of Atonement: 'Take your case directly to God – start at the top!'

After the churchmen's pontification, a crane had collapsed onto the Wren church in the City of London, breaking its rose window, just as the rose window of York Minster had been destroyed in the fire following the pontifications of the Bishop of Durham.

She met David by Alec's street on the frosty road.

'Are you going to see Alec?'

'Yes.'

'How is he?'

'O, you know. Up and down. Looks like a skeleton. He tries to keep happy within himself.'

'Give them all my love.'

'I will.'

...I should get a card for them, she thought. And confectionery stockings for the children...

Waiting to see the specialist amidst older couples, families with children (despite there being a crèche, for this was a new, well-equipped hospital), she saw one man supporting himself on a 4-footed metal stick, and a young, beautifully dressed and made-up girl: unaccompanied, also waiting; serene but for one foot spasmodically beating its own uncontrolled twitch.

One minute you were just in bed, turning to read a book on your right side; the next, a pain, a pea-sized lump, felt first by Bill and then by the GP.

She was weighed, including shoes and jumper and all but her anorak. They were laughing, 'Not too many in today!'

After forty minutes she was sitting with the consultant.

'Is there any history of breast cancer in your family?'

'My mother died of breast cancer. So did my aunt.'

'Your mother's sister?'

'Yes.'

'Well it is very common. One in every twelve women. Most people don't have to go very far back in their families to find cases...'

'In my case that is one hundred per cent.'

She undressed for the consultant and agreed to the presence of several students.

'...a small cyst... nothing to worry about... just see if I can puncture it now with a needle...'

Leaving the hospital skipping and singing, laughing out loud, as though God were saying, 'Get out of here and get on with living – *I'm* not ready for *you* yet.'

Waiting for a bus outside the hospital, she re-encountered the toothless old woman who had crossed the road next to her on her arrival. 'I'm waiting fe me dentures. Didn't I see you on the way in? O have I had a time! They squashed my poor titty down between these plates till it looked like something'd been through a bacon-slicer. Aye, you can laugh' – to the two young men in jeans and trainers, shockedly guffawing at what they overheard. 'You wait till they do it to you down there!'

The bus came and she climbed upstairs, sitting at the front on the single seat with an amiable woman and child across the gangway, flung almost on top of them as the bus swayed, hearing her own ringing laughter.

DROWNED

A Novella

DROWNED

'*One* picture of a man with a drowned toddler in his arms, wading out of the sea!

That picture is pole-axing the whole nation!

Look at all these politicians telling us we must take more refugees!

One drowned three-year old has sent them all into hysterics.

You're not homeless in this country!

You haven't got a kid with no place in school!

You're not a woman in this country threatened with Sharia law *on her own doorstep!* Get real!'

She looked up from the set to accept a cup of tea from her daughter.

'That one man preaching Sharia law at me in my own garden changed my whole attitude to life.

Now I see *Muslim* not as that smiling man delivering bricks for my patio on that roasting hot day during Ramadan, refusing even a glass of water, but that ranting immigrant treating me *automatically* as some inferior being over whom he held dominion – in my *own* country, on my *own* land!'

She stared back at the set.

'They weren't in Syria!

They were in *Turkey!*

They paid 5000 Euro to a smuggler!

They got into a *tiny* boat to cross to Kos, the smuggler jumped off, the dinghy capsized – and now everyone is whingeing that the kid died!

Look at this! Look at this! On this … television… Ferocious

loud clapping behind that Scottish cow as she talks with a break in her voice, "We *can't* walk by…"

O aren't you all clever!

Aren't you all patting yourselves on the back!

They'll all whinge and bellyache like mad when we do get Sharia law in this country!

And they *demand* it *as a right!*

Germany! Germany!

Why don't they move to an Islamic country!

They are *Muslims!*

I'm not a *Muslim!*

I don't want Sharia Law!

They talk about it in relation to other religions – "What about Jewish refugees in the war?"

The *Jews* don't want to convert us all to Judaism!

The *Jews* don't want to repress British women!'

Picking up a paper and reading out: *'Family of Drowned Boys Were Trying to Join Relatives For New Life in Canada.* So instead of looking again at the paperwork he shoves his family into an unseaworthy boat!

Look at it! Every blessed paper is like this!

Blessed bleeding hearts! – They're wallowing in it. They love it – registering how good they are.

Look at this!

Piece in this one about "online lynchers."

Same as this immigration farce.

There's this… narcissistic delight in punishing others.

And that radio! Someone blethering on about the doomed toddler's "Faith and hope in the future."

What "faith and hope in the future"!

Kids don't have "faith and hope in the future," they just

have egotistical *life.'*

She said at lunch-time, as she washed the pots:

'Wanted a better life for his kids.

Why didn't they stay in Turkey and apply again for Canada?

With relatives there, he might have got in.

The father panicked, I suppose.

And we all pay for panicking.

But now he's got two dead sons and a wife buried in Syria, instead of a family in Turkey.'

She dried her hands on the tea-towel.

'They are so *demanding*.

That's what worries me.

Men who *demand* in his way, as though for their rights, are just the ones who *would* impose Sharia law on their host country – as their *right.'*

Responding to an announcement from the radio: 'Cameron is saying we will take refugees from their camps.

Well that's logical.

From the start, he said that we ought to help people in their own area – giving so much overseas' aid that they've started blethering in *this* country!

What's the point of encouraging people to *start out* on these journeys, *encouraging* people-traffickers?

When he did propose military intervention, he was shot down!

Now I reckon they'll listen.

All because of one panicky father and one drowned boy.'

Her teenage daughter joined to watch the news with her.

'Look at all those Germans, how welcoming – toys for the

kids, handshakes for the men...'

'Well of course they're welcoming! They killed 6 million Jews!'

'We took Jews. In the war.'

'You're not going to get *Jews* planting bombs on the underground in London!'

'They're not planting bombs. Someone's got to help them.'

'You've just got into uni. You've got your own life to lead.'

'I could take a gap year.'

'You are not going to Europe to help those refugees and that's final!'

'They've only got one life. Someone's got to help them.'

'*You've* got one life and you'd better live it now! What do you think they want to come over here for? To get the sort of opportunities you're talking about throwing away!'

Her husband entered to hear his wife explode:

'She wants to give up University to help these migrants!'

'At least I've got a heart. I might not have a degree but I've got a heart!'

'Got a heart! What do you think *that* means! Yelling away, telling other people they're heartless! Got a heart!

Bleeding-heart politicians! O spare me! When I was young, a student, I lived in a heavily-immigrant area. I said once to my friend, isn't it good to be able to rent a place so close to central London? She said, yes, it's all right for you, but think of the people who'd bought houses here earlier.

Everything's changed since then anyway. All sorts of places that only had Jewish refugees from the war now have loads of different cultures. Where I grew up, in the North, you never saw a black face – an Asian shopkeeper, even a Chinese. I think they did get a Chinese chippy, after I left. – And it wasn't all peace and quiet then, when I was a student. There was a race-riot then. An Asian student was killed. Outside my door. I took part in the community march. Carried the banner past the top of the street – my street – where he'd been killed. Vanessa Redgrave marched at the back. A priest stood in his church door, cassock billowing, waiting for the bride – but you couldn't get through, there was no traffic moving…'

'Someone on the radio's just said they thought the father was partly responsible.'

'Well yes, I do think that. Putting his family into a tiny boat. They weren't in Syria! They were in Turkey! Darwin was right: survival of the fittest…'

'Darwin never said that!'

She continued, talking over her daughter, 'Look, you're going to have millions! This isn't like Jews in the war. The Kindertransport. You've got whole nations, whole populations…'

'Amy's mother's talking of taking one in. You could put one up in my room, when I'm at uni…'

'Listen, my girl, you want to invite total strangers from God knows where to live in your house, you start earning and buy your own house, don't go inviting them into mine!'

'Amy's mother…'

'I don't give a fig about Amy's mother! Amy's mother can do what she likes! My name's on those deeds…'

'So's mine,' said her father.

'You can't do anything without me! And I say no. N.O.'

They settle again to watch the television.

'Bleeding-heart liberals! O spare me!'

The girl imitates her mother's catch-phrases in sotto, making her father laugh.

'They blether on about Hungary, going all po-faced – the Germans *told* Hungary: make sure they're all registered by you before you let them through! Then: O, O, there's too many, they can't all be registered, let them all come! Now Merkel's saying: Germany cannot resolve this refugee crisis alone. Of *course* they can't! It's *continent*-fuls!'

The girl started, 'That's what makes it a *crisis...*'

Her mother talked over her. 'Half of them aren't refugees! They're bullies! O, we won't stay here! *Germany! Germany! –* We won't stay in Calais! They're in blessed France! Who's persecuting them in *France! –* There's no housing, no schools, for those here already! Mind you, your Granny was taught in classes of 50, and she passed her 11+.'

'2 2s are 4,

2 4s are 8...'

The daughter stood, imitating the learn-by-rote system.

'Joe public!

They know it all!

Your Granny once lived in a politician's house. She answered the phone for him sometimes. It was all, "Do it now, do it yesterday, *you* are *our* servants, *we're* the ones who vote!" The rudest were old men: "Why should I talk to you! *You're* not my MP!" She'd only been trying to give him a message! She'd get frantic phone calls about refugees: "He's at the airport! They're deporting him now!" He'd get back from the House only to find, "O, don't worry, that's all been sorted out!"

Overpaid politicians! Christ! *I* wouldn't do that job for all the tea in China!'

'You know it all, don't you? You've got all the answers!'

'It's called being old.'

Well-covered but not fleshy, an accountant who had not

quite made the actuarial exams, her father was an amiable man, used to the bickering between his wife and daughter, sometimes even quietly amused.

His daughter was asking his wife, 'How would you feel? If it was me?'

His wife made the appropriate knife movement. 'I'd slit my throat.'

Her mother could not get over the man in the garden.

'In my own garden!

In my own house!

"What you do out here? Where is husband? Husband should be here. You with childrens, in kitchen!"

No man speaks to me like that!

Not even my own father!

Never in my life!

Sharia law!

On my own doorstep!

On my own land!

I mean, look at it! Round here! London's leafy suburbs! We're hardly a deprived area! We're not suppressing anyone! They're not sunk in poverty! If it's like this round here, it's going on everywhere! What must it be like in South London, in the North!

All I'd done was say, "Nice day, isn't it!"

The sun was out. He was delivering leaflets. He'd just pushed a leaflet through my door.

Gardening, in my own front garden! *Nothing* to provoke him. He starts. These men, on this television, going on, *Germany! Germany!* Do you think *they* aren't the same? Do you think *they* wouldn't do it!'

'That's just one man...'

'What do you know? *You're* not a woman! No *man* has a right to open his face on this subject! Not Cameron! Not the Prince of Wales! O-oh! It makes me so *angry!* On my own doorstep! On my *own land!'*

She turned to her interrupting daughter, 'Yes, I did buy a Koran. Started reading it. No, I haven't read it all. I've read more of it than anyone else round here – all these pontificators. So far it's just Old Testament, with "Muhammad says."

Yes, it does.

Look at it. It's upstairs.

Even got the Arabic, if you're talking about going off to Syria.

You will find a part-read Koran in this house.

After that incident in the front garden.

Wanted to know what it was all about.

"Knowledge is power!" I said, waving it in Waterstones as I marched out.'

She paused in the silence, resuming:

'But, you know, nobody's thought this through:

What if they do come over here and you do get inter-Muslim violence? Sunni against Shia? That could happen. Inter-Muslim warfare? In this city?

We've already *had* 9/11, 7/7! I'm not projecting horrors out of thin air! How would you feel if one of *them* took your daughter!

And – think on this – What about paranoia?

People always feel they're picked on.

"O, it's because we're black – we're picked on – stop and search – the police stop us."

When I was a girl in this city, the police stopped me! They

stopped Amy! They say they're looking for runaways – they accuse you of being a prostitute! They've done it to me! They did it to Amy.'

'Amy thinks you're a racist.'

'*Amy* says I'm a racist! Tell Amy I've had root canal treatment from Muslim dentists more often than she's had hot dinners, and in my book there's no one you trust more than the man who is holding a drill up your skull! Go and look at that Koran. Take it to show Amy – I'll bet *she's* never seen it. It's even got the Arabic – you'll need that, if you're off to Syria. The pair of you. I know a bit of the Old and a bit of the New and a bit of the Koran. I once read a book called *What Jews Believe...*'

'Those books between them have killed more people...'

'Now *there's* an original thought! You put your money on Dawkins, do you? Him and his crowd. The ones who call all the rest *childish* for some sort of belief in God? More evil in human beings, I'd say.'

'You can't have *evil* without religion!'

The television showed limbless bandaged men, burnt children in hospitals, weeping, and curly heads gazing straight at camera.

She sat for a moment in silence before declaring,

'So you think it isn't *evil*

not to educate girls,

to cut them,

to throw acid in someone's face,

to burn them for insufficient dowry,

to marry them off,

deny them rights,

to claim them half the worth of men?

Is that what you think? Eh?'

She said this looking straight at the television, watching Syrian ruins and transit camps and refugee camp squalor, small round blue tents and hordes at stations, men behind wire fences which made them look caged. Men clambering into the backs of lorries whose doors swung open. Men climbing out over the tops of tankers, under police eyes.

'People aren't just groups! They're *individuals*...'

'Well *I* wasn't, was I? In my own front garden! I was in that group: *women!*'

'All Muslim men aren't like that. It isn't like that for all Muslim women.'

'No. It isn't. I've lived next door to Muslim women – and Hindu women – who relish their power. Relish their place in the family. But if you're not like that, if you're not Mama Mia...'

'Well you've just said it. Italian...'

Italian girls aren't denied education! Italian women aren't kept out of jobs and university. *Italian* women aren't not free to leave the country! I've known Muslim women happy with their lot, I've seen Muslim women in burkas, with their families, congregating round Selfridge's ice-cream parlour, spoon-feeding their kids – they *like* this, they might even choose it. I've also, when I was a student, worked with a Muslim girl who sat at her keyboard, crying, tears streaming down her face, day after day, as she tried to work – her father had stopped her marrying the man of her choice. The man she'd grown up thinking she would marry. All the rest of the family were in favour, his own brother even wrote to him, but he, he was the father, he had the power, he was the only one who counted, he could say no. *I'm* free, I can go out today, if I choose to be a Muslim after I've read that Koran I can go out today and convert. But *they* can't! These girls can't convert back! They can't pull out. Tied by birth! Tied to some father's apron-strings – his whip-hand...'

The girl and her father exchanged grins.

'I don't think you'd ever be chained to mine!'

'All over the world, in all sorts of cultures, women are...'

'And why should HE ever do it to ME! I am in my own fucking country in my own fucking garden of my *own fucking house!*

She was blazing.

'Next thing he'll be cutting my cunt off. What do you *think* it is? FGM?'

'Ow! Ow!'

Her mother had her hand to her mouth.

'You and your endodentistry!' she laughed. 'You're the only one who calls it that.'

'Didn't know root canal work was endodentistry till I heard one of the dentists say it...'

'One of your Muslim dentists!'

'Yes, he was a Muslim.' She was rubbing the side of her mouth. 'My nose is numb.'

She made tea as her face thawed. She sat on the couch with her daughter, nursing the cup against her cheek.

'I wouldn't have allowed my own father to speak to me like that and he was no pushover, believe me.

I've always been Better Dead Than Red.

My God, Better Dead Than Sharia! – What would have happened, if your Father had been there? Inciting racial hatred, that's what that is – *they're* inciting racial hatred! Provoking fist-fights.'

She drank from the cup, swilling the warm tea gingerly

against her numbness.

'What did you do?'

'I was gobsmacked. That was the trouble. You never *believe*, round here, you never suspect such things could even be *thought!*'

She swilled more tea. 'You see, that's what I mean. They don't even *suspect.* It is *intrinsic.* They don't even suspect they're doing wrong. They think they are right, they think they *can* come here and say such things, they think it's their *right* to be obeyed by women. There's no everyone-has-their-own-beliefs. Not in their book.'

'Christians did it. In the Crusades.'

'Yes, Christians did do it. Jews aren't like this! Nobody does it now! Not in England. But no, no, we must all be Muslims! That's what we're importing!'

'They're not all like that. It's only happened once.'

'It wasn't you it happened to. Turned my world on its head. – And it's never swung back!'

She drank her tea.

'It's one thing to respect everyone's religion. It's another to have them disrespecting yours.

– Not even your religion, but *you!*

For being what you are!

Just for being a woman.

A non-Muslim woman.

That's what *you'd* be, over, there.'

'I don't think we're going. That was just a joke, really. But Amy's mother is talking of having some refugees in her house. A child. Or a family.'

'Your father'll be glad you're not going. He worries, even if he doesn't show.'

Her daughter said from the kitchen, 'Women are used like that in many cultures...'

'But not in this country! In this country, women run banks, women are in charge of university departments! I've never even been a feminist. I always have preferred men to women. I enjoy men's talk, I like men's advice, I respect your father. Don't know the first thing about finance. Your father is in charge of all that.'

'Amy's mother says you wanted a boy.'

'Yes, I would have liked a boy, but when you came along you were such a beautiful little girl...'

Her father came in, laughing. 'Can't argue with that!'

Some Euro politician was saying, 'If we do not cope with this crisis, it will cost us not only credibility, it will cost us great grievance as Europeans.'

'Well *find* an answer! There isn't! Whole continents moving!'

'Look how happy they all are! To be in Europe! Falling to their knees: "Thank God I made it!" *Delight!* They all show *delight!* Europe is Paradise!'

'They only used to cross at night. Now they cross by day as well.'

Euphoria at being in Europe.

'Chaos!'

A television voice proclaimed, 'The Greeks can't even give them a lift before they have been registered, otherwise they can be accused of trafficking.'

US Green Card system advocated.

The girl exulted. 'Look at them! "I'm happy!" "I'm safe! I'm safe at last!"'

'*Who* is fighting ISIS?'

'Good people, bad people – we're all just *people!*'

'Some are born good and some are born bad, but we can all hurt each other.'

'What about being nice to each other?'

'You're my daughter. I just don't want anyone hurting you.'

The television was quoting figures, of allocations to different lands.

'Look at the Saudis! As rich as Croesus. All that oil money. Massive lands. They won't take any. And they're *Muslims!* Truest words in the Bible. Truest words ever written. *For he that hath, to him shall be given; and he that hath not, from him shall be taken even that which he hath.* I'm not advocating! I'm just saying: it *is.*'

A well-built boy, on the television, trying to talk in English to the BBC man. Beside him, his mother, tucked into her white hijab. The child was the image of his mother. "You English. You help me please. Get to England."

'Him I like. Him I would give a home to. Not these ingratiating curly-mops.'

The BBC man explained that Britain was not taking refugees from those who had paid traffickers. The boy's head slumped to his hands.

On the anniversary of 9/11, Obama says he will take 10,000.

Hungarian scenes, 14 years after 9/11 to the day:

A sick child in one camp, separated from her mother; crowds of refugees in wire cages, even more scrabbling for sandwiches, food thrown over the wire; police in masks; dirt and filth in the camps.

'People are being treated like animals.'

'But *what* are they *supposed* to do! It's not even supposed to be a camp, it's meant to be a place where people can catch buses... the Red Cross *are* there! These Hungarians are not making people suffer on *purpose!* How would other countries cope? What are they supposed to do? What do you do, if you are overwhelmed by numbers, if the numbers are too great, what are you supposed to do!

It's all right talking about kiddies slithering around in muddy puddles.

They're lying down under the buses...

Have you *read* some of these articles on Islamic schools, on what goes on *in this country.* It's all Islamic studies – get the GCSEs out of the way, so they can concentrate on Islam. *Obedience.* That's all it is. For Muslim women. *Do as you are told!* I've never listened to anyone, even my own father, when I was a kid – now I'm supposed to kowtow to some religion – not mine! – to some Islamic *man!*

Tolerance is said to be a good thing. Tolerance of evil is a sin.

To have a *total stranger,* chastise me, with Sharia law, on my own land! – Yes, it is already over here – we do now have Sharia courts!

Listen, it's not just the Koran up there, it's *cuttings!* Here you are! I'll show you! Pieces on Islamic schools – in this country! "Some pupils do not know the difference between Sharia and British law."

No, you don't believe me, you think I'm making it up! I was out there, doing the roses. He started in. "Where is your husband! Your husband should be at the front. You must be indoors, cooking." In my own freehold house in my own garden. Said without hesitation or qualm, without *suspicion* that he might be wrong! O I wrote to Theresa May. It was just before the election. I said, you're really going to lose out to UKIP if you don't sort this out. No, she never replied.

For a woman, it is fascism. Women have no rights. Some women like it – responsibility is taken out of their hands, their men have to look after them – or at least make the decisions. I don't want to live in a cocoon! No, no, this will not wash! Islam is a man's religion. Men can cut women, control them, destroy their daughter's lives, forbidding them or forcing them to marry.

I don't care what religion people are, but *this* religion seeks to destroy *me*. Believe you me, there are some adult Muslim men who think that Sharia law *is* the law of England!

And *they* have the nerve to say that *they* are persecuted – a *witch-hunt!* You can't say anything, you see. You mustn't talk like this – it's racialism! Racialist! To tell the truth! There are people who do want Sharia law in this country. And they'll fight for it! Anyone who thinks that they can sit back and this will not happen is living in Cloud Cuckoo Land.'

O he turned me.
100%.
I'd never been a feminist before.
If that can happen round here, then what the hell is going on in the rest of the country?
She showed her daughter cuttings dating back from months before the crisis: ISIS invading countries, beheading people, beheading children; children captured and turned so that their families feared their return, feared they would kill them. Reports from English Islamic journalists on what the veil did to women. British ex-soldiers fighting jihadists. UK acid attacks.
Her daughter made no comment. She sensed reluctance to

believe. She said, in resentment:

'If you want Sharia law, go to a country that has Sharia law. Don't think you can bring it to *this* country!'

Slavery in the UK. Trafficked women. Columnists' articles trying to deal with this. 'They can't deal with it. They won't bite the bullet. This is our sole country! We are not immigrants, we have no other place to go to, and we are credited with having no rights!

Everybody goes on about rights – rights to free speech, as they try to stop other people enjoying their freedom. With rights go responsibilities. I *will not* be subjected to Sharia law *in this country!*'

She said, picking up a cutting, 'Here, look, here's the article about Dawood – "Translator of the most popular English-language version of the Koran." That's the one – but mine's got the Arabic. Jewish bloke. Letters all the time from people prompted to convert to Islam by his Koran. Well that's all fine, that's as it should be – but give people freedom, give them the right to choose!

"Misogynistic male barristers" – is it misogyny? To want to see someone's face? In court? If it's life or death you're judging, haven't you the right to see the reactions on a witness' face?

Sharia law *made* me a feminist!

Men don't know.

Men have no idea.

It's quite different for men.

Men have all the rights, men only have to deal with other men – and any fit, educated, entitled Englishman, who has power and makes decisions: he'd pit himself in any one-to-one against another man. This isn't evil or viciousness, it's not anti-feminism but blindness: he stands where he stands, he's never had to contemplate what this means from any other point of view.

Cutting, controlling; decreeing choices; dictating the life that a woman *will* have.

I've worked with a woman whose life was ruined by her father's refusal to let her marry; lived where girls were killed by family members, for "family honour;" wives burnt at the stove or scalded for insufficient dowry.

It was the *way* he did it.

No *conception* that he could cause offence.

Just *completely* as if it were his *right!*

So sure he was a man, *in charge, he* could dictate to any woman what she must do – his utter belief that *he* had the power, *he* must be obeyed!

They feel this *must* be the law in this country, act as though it is; would impose it, if questioned.

It is *their* law, at home, and *they* want it *here.*

Give not an inch! Do *not* indulge *this!* No Englishman – or woman – can put his foot down hard enough!'

She snatched up another cutting that caught her eye, thrusting it at her daughter.

'*This* columnist's right! Time of Charlie Hebdo! We *have* operated a Muslim double-standard!'

Her daughter picked up another cutting. 'You talk as though this is all Muslims! Here's a piece saying how moderate Muslims hate this!'

Her mother said, ignoring her: 'Feminists bellyached about MCPs in this country and now they're too scared to stand up and oppose Sharia!'

Terror attacks in France. …Clash of civilizations… letters about not looking problems in the face.

'If it's true Prince Charles thinks there should be tolerance of Sharia in this country I'd draw a cartoon myself of him sporting a T-shirt: *Je suis Charlie.*'

Headline: *Muslim students fail to honour dead*

Teach freedom of speech to save from extremists

Charles finds Jihad 'bewildering' headline in The Times

Mosques urged to tackle tough issues

'Muslims aren't the only ones who can take offence. No pork in schools, separating the sexes at lectures. If you don't want to live in England with English laws, go and live somewhere else.'

Cartoonists right to fight blasphemy

'I'm not alive to please you. I'm alive to please myself. Who are you? You're nothing to me.

They think their religion and their desires and their needs supersede yours. Because they think this of women, they think it of all men!

Islamic Sharia Council set up in London in 1982 ... "Religious law does not create men and women the same" ... "We are talking about people's right to practise their own faith." *WHAT ABOUT **MINE!**'*

She had never seen her mother so angry.

She had picked up and read out another cutting.

'*Veiled. Traded in marriage. Genitally mutilated.* – THIS is the religious faith these bastards want in this country!'

Jihadist let son hold severed head

There is a battle for the soul of Islam

'It's not being won.'

Myth that Islam is a religion of peace

Preacher who praised 7/7 cannot be deported

Woman who survived 7/7 talks of her shock as a Muslim to learn that the bombers were Muslim:

'It clearly says the Koran: "To kill one innocent life is as though you have killed the whole of mankind."'

A note in her mother's hand: 'This page is filed *in* the Koran.'

Articles had begun appearing about sectarian hatred amongst British Muslims.

Her father agreed: 'Hate preachers – that's no good to anybody.'

She had brought her mother's Koran folder downstairs and sat, looking through the cuttings.

At the time of the Calais crisis, someone had written: 'Bring in ID cards!' Once in the country, they feel that they can't be deported... Across the top, her mother had written: 'You should hear them in Greece! They talk of nothing but their *rights*. Poor Greeks can barely help themselves. This is not poor despairing migrants, this is *greed!*' Across one article she had written, 'These people do not know what poverty is if they can pay £800! ... They're not persecuted in *FRANCE!*'

70th anniversary of Hiroshima: *Nuclear option holds no fear for ISIS*

'Islamic extremism is a cancer spreading round the world.'

Danger from 'anti-British Muslims.'

Koran encourages rape...

Women-only Mosques led by male Imams

In her mother's hand: Mohammad the most common name for boys born in London. We are a democracy. One day they won't need to fight to get Sharia law: they'll vote for it.

Ravages of war keep 14 million from school

The famous picture of the drowned Syrian toddler, lifted from the sea.

Christian groups embrace Syrian refugees in Austria

Boy clutching teddy, on rail-track

Case for air-strikes against IS
City shows way with refugee appeals
Merkel 'naïve'
They can build fences but we will get over them
Woman on hands and knees amongst men with guns
What Brits really think about taking refugees
We're full! says Munich – 40,000 enter Germany
Cameron in a camp: Refugees from Syria will have a good warm
home in the UK

'Amy's mother's refugee has turned up.'
'O yes. What's he like?'
'Don't know. He doesn't speak any English.'
'How old?'
'Twenty.'
'That was quick. I thought it would take longer.'
'He's studying, that's why.'
'What subject?'
'Pure maths.'
'That's good!' exclaimed her father. 'Perhaps he'll be an actuary!'
'What's that?'
'Very rich!'
'Is he from Syria?'
'Think so. One of the camps. The Red Cross or something got him here – they found out he was good at maths.'
'Is Amy helping him learn English?'
'She takes him shopping. He's whiz at those self-service things.'
'I sat the Actuarial exams.'
'Your Dad nearly passed. Only failed one subject.'

'Get his name in *The Times!*'

'He loves maths. He's never off his iPhone. He's downloaded this special app…'

'Well he'll be right at home here, then. That's all you see on the tube these days – kids on their smartphones, playing Candy Crush.'

'Well he won't be playing that!'

She went round to see Amy, but Amy must be out. She let herself in, round the back.

The refugee was there, fraught, jabbing his machine.

'Not work! Not work! Not work!'

'It must need charging. Have you got its lead?'

He was not listening to her.

'Needs charging! Have you got its lead? Re-charge… you have to have the right lead. Is it in your room?' She was showing him the socket. 'Re-charge! You must have the right lead.' She led the way upstairs. A lead snaked from one of the hall sockets. She was on the floor, examining the plugged-in lead. 'I don't think this is Apple; I think this is for Amy's Samsung. You must be careful – if you plug the wrong thing in with the wrong lead, you can get a shock, set fire to the house. That's what they say with e-cigs, anyway. Not that anyone smokes in this house.'

The confused boy did not understand, jabbing his dead machine.

'Do you smoke?

Smoke?

Do you smoke?'

She kept patting her lips with two fingers. He thought he was being asked to kiss her.

She is in his arms.
He tries to comfort.
She keeps coming out with these juddered thoughts.

She said:
'O it just ends.
You might be still alive but you're not alive.
It just ends.'

She said:
'People think it's brave.
Of course it's not.
It's just stupid.'

She said:
'Well there isn't any way out.
It's all stupid.
It follows its natural course till it comes to an end.'

She said:
'People pretend.
It's better than it is.
For other people.
Until it isn't *for them.*'

She said:
'That man.
Who took his kid into the sea.
Who saw his child drown.
At least he had *choice!*'

'We brought up a beautiful girl!
She's gone!'
He held her to him.
'I can't give her clothes to Oxfam!'
'I'll do that.'
She said, in his arms, 'I knew this would happen!'
'That was only one man…'
'It only takes one man to kill my daughter.'

'Don't stand there, woman!'

She was in Sainsbury's, buying bread.

She could not believe her ears.

She was being told off, by a tiny child.

'Did you just say something?'

'Yes.'

'What did you say?'

'Don't stand there, woman. You shouldn't be…'

'How *dare* you! Talk to me like that! How *dare* you! How dare you think that you can talk to *any* woman like that! You're a child! Behave! Don't ever talk like that to anybody ever again!'

Incensed, she walked on, then went back.

The father was there. She rebuked the child before him.

'I've no right to be here! How dare you! How dare you!'

The father wanted to stop her.

'Talk to me…' he was being placatory. 'Don't talk to me in front of my child…'

'No! I will not listen to you! I will not listen to him! No! He is wrong! This must be stopped! I am not having Sharia law in this country!'

'I'm not bad really,' the boy said.

'Yes you are! You have *got* to learn that you *cannot* talk to women like that in this country! I will not be put down! No! I won't listen to you! I won't listen to him! I come to Sainsbury's to buy bread and there's a 4-year old *kid* preaching Sharia law at me!'

All griefs differ; but one thing they have in common.
She's dead – she *isn't!*
Hit. In the street.
Hit. At work.
Hit. Half-way up the stairs.

No way round.
Gone on too long.
Let this stop now.
She's dead – she *isn't!*

The man fell totally silent.
He missed his wife's ceaseless chatter, her endless dark humour, never bitter, the banter which she and his daughter had shared.
Her grief had swept her away as totally as his child.

And there were no stages to this grief, it did not go up and down, it was just black, solidly black, black as the waters of the canal into which she had thrown herself and drowned.

THE END

www.ingramcontent.com/pod-product-compliance
Lightning Source LLC
Chambersburg PA
CBHW050149110726

47898CB00008B/2727